PUFFIN BOOKS

DOUBTING THOMAS

Morris Gleitzman grew up in England and went to live in Australia when he was sixteen. He worked as a frozen-chicken thawer, sugar-mill rolling-stock unhooker, fashion-industry trainee, department-store Santa, TV producer, newspaper columnist and screenwriter. Then he had a wonderful experience. He wrote a novel for young people. Now he's one of the bestselling children's authors in Australia. He lives in Melbourne, but visits Britain regularly. His many books include *Two Weeks with the Queen*, *Water Wings*, *Bumface*, *Boy Overboard*, *Toad Rage* and *Once*.

Books by Morris Gleitzman

Morris Gleitzman

DOUBTING THOMAS

PUFFIN

PUFFIN BOOKS

Published by the Penguin Group
Penguin Books Ltd, 80 Strand, London WC2R ORL, England
Penguin Group (USA) Inc., 375 Hudson Street, New York, New York 10014, USA
Penguin Group (Canada), 90 Eglinton Avenue East, Suite 700, Toronto, Ontario, Canada M4P 2Y3
(a division of Pearson Penguin Canada Inc.)
Penguin Ireland, 25 St Stephen's Green, Dublin 2, Ireland (a division of Penguin Books Ltd)
Penguin Group (Australia), 250 Camberwell Road, Camberwell, Victoria 3124, Australia
(a division of Pearson Australia Group Pty Ltd)
Penguin Books India Pvt Ltd, 11 Community Centre, Panchsheel Park,
New Delhi – 110 017, India
Penguin Group (NZ), 67 Apollo Drive, Rosedale, North Shore 0632, New Zealand
(a division of Pearson New Zealand Ltd)
Penguin Books (South Africa) (Pty) Ltd, 24 Sturdee Avenue, Rosebank,
Johannesburg 2196, South Africa

Penguin Books Ltd, Registered Offices: 80 Strand, London WC2R ORL, England

puffinbooks.com

First published by Penguin Group (Australia), a division of Pearson Australia Group Pty Ltd 2006
Published in Great Britain in Puffin Books 2007

3

Text copyright © Creative Input Pty Ltd, 2006
All rights reserved

The moral right of the author and illustrator has been asserted

Set in Minion
Made and printed in England by Clays Ltd, St Ives plc

British Library Cataloguing in Publication Data
A CIP catalogue record for this book is available from the British Library

ISBN: 978–0–141–32295–7

www.greenpenguin.co.uk

Mixed Sources
Product group from well managed
forests and other controlled sources
www.fsc.org Cert no. SA-COC-1592
© 1996 Forest Stewardship Council

Penguin Books is committed to a sustainable future
for our business, our readers and our planet.
The book in your hands is made from paper
certified by the Forest Stewardship Council.

For Tilly and Dexter

Thomas sat in the doctor's waiting room, trying not to panic about his arm.

It wasn't looking good. A red stain was seeping through the bandage.

Oops, thought Thomas. I think I used too much jam.

Mum was always saying he put too much jam on his toast. Now he'd put too much on his arm as well.

Lucky there weren't any other patients in the waiting room.

Or flies.

Thomas gave the bandage a couple of prods. More jam leaked out.

He glanced at Alisha to see if she'd noticed that his arm was looking less like a stab wound and more like an after-school snack.

She was busy texting.

That's one good thing about big sisters, thought Thomas. They only notice their mobiles.

'You might as well take that stupid bandage off,' said Alisha, not looking up from her phone. 'That fake injury's not fooling me and it won't fool the doctor.'

Thomas sighed.

That was the bad thing about big sisters. Even when they failed year ten science, they still thought they were medical experts.

Thomas decided to try and sound indignant.

'What do you mean, fake injury?' he said. 'I told you, I stabbed myself with the fruit knife trying to open a box of Cheezels. If you hadn't got home from school when you did, I could be dead by now.'

'Yeah,' said Alisha, frowning at the phone, thumbs moving fast. 'Dead from a tomato sauce overdose.'

Thomas sighed again.

He should have known he couldn't fool Alisha.

'It's jam,' he muttered.

She grinned, but didn't look up.

Thomas noticed a tingle of something in his chest that felt a little bit like gratitude.

He had to admit he was pretty lucky to have a sister like Alisha. She probably knew all along it wasn't a real stab wound, and had still come to the doctor's with him when he'd asked her.

I wish I'd been more generous, thought Thomas. I wish I'd bribed her with four jelly snakes instead of just two.

Still grinning, Alisha leaned over and prodded his bandage. Then she licked her finger.

'Yum,' she said. 'Raspberry.'

'Do you mind?' said Thomas, but his heart wasn't in it.

Suddenly he wanted to tell Alisha the truth. The real reason he'd faked an arm wound. The real reason he needed to see the doctor.

But he didn't. It was too embarrassing.

Plus he couldn't speak right now. The feeling in his chest was much stronger, and it wasn't gratitude. He was having another attack.

Thomas closed his eyes and tried to stay calm. He tried to remember what number attack this was. The ninth today. Which made it one hundred and fifty-seven since the attacks began two weeks ago.

After a few moments, as always, his chest went back to normal.

Thomas opened his eyes.

Alisha was still looking at him.

'I was eleven once,' she said. 'I know what it's like when your body starts going weird. You don't have to be embarrassed. It happens to everyone.'

No it doesn't, thought Thomas. Not what I've got.

'What is it you're worried about?' said Alisha. 'Hair in strange places? Rude dreams? Funny-shaped willy?'

Thomas didn't know where to look.

'Perhaps,' said Alisha quietly, 'I can help.'

Thomas stared at her.

He'd never heard that concerned and understanding tone in her voice before. Not when she was speaking to him.

'Come on,' said Alisha gently. 'What is it?'

Thomas decided to tell her, even though he'd vowed never to tell a non-doctor anything private about himself ever again.

Before he could say a word, there was a loud thumping on the waiting-room windows.

Thomas looked up and his insides sank.

It was Rocco Fusilli and the boys from school. They were pressing themselves against the glass and pulling faces at Thomas and rubbing their chests in a way they obviously thought was hilarious.

Thomas pretended not to see them, and desperately hoped Alisha hadn't seen them either.

She had.

'Cretins,' she said, glaring at the boys. 'That school should get the pest exterminator in.' Then she looked at Thomas and her face softened. 'I'm guessing, seeing those lower life forms out there, that you're worried about your chest.'

Thomas blushed. And nodded.

'Itchy nipples,' he mumbled.

Alisha stared at him. Then she stared at the front of his t-shirt.

'Itchy nipples,' she said.

Thomas could see she was struggling not to smile.

It's alright for you, he thought. You're a girl. You're allowed to have nipples.

'How itchy?' she asked.

Thomas wanted to say very, very, very itchy, but he didn't because a woman had just walked into the waiting room and was sitting down opposite them. He nudged Alisha to keep quiet.

Alisha leaned towards him.

She obviously wasn't going to keep quiet.

Thomas glanced anxiously at the woman and tried to look as though he didn't know Alisha.

'It's normal,' Alisha whispered to him. 'I used to get it. When my boobs were growing.'

Thomas felt ill.

He wanted to point out to Alisha that (a) he was a boy (b) his boobs weren't growing and (c) he hoped they'd stay that way. But he kept quiet because the woman was staring at him.

Just like she will later on, thought Thomas miserably, if I turn into a girl.

Alisha was glaring through the window at the boys again.

'How do that lot know?' she said.

'I told them,' admitted Thomas. 'After soccer one day. To see if any of them had ever had it.'

'You idiot,' said Alisha, about three times louder than she needed to, in Thomas's opinion. 'Never tell cretins anything personal. They'll use it to get you, everybody knows that.'

Thomas nodded sadly.

He knew that now. The day after he told Rocco and the team about his itchy nipples, the whole school was whispering and giggling about Thomas Gulliver turning into a girl.

Alisha stood up.

'I'm just going outside for a sec,' she said.

Oh no, thought Thomas.

He could tell from her face what she was planning to do. Make Rocco Fusilli and the rest of the team wish they'd gone to soccer practice instead.

'Don't,' pleaded Thomas. 'You'll only make it worse.'

'I'm just going out to use my phone,' said Alisha. 'I can't get good reception in here.'

Thomas knew that wasn't true. She'd been getting texts from her boyfriend Garth for the last ten minutes. Thomas had peeked and seen words like 'lve' and 'sxy'.

He stood up to try and stop Alisha but it was no good. His nipples were killing him again and he needed both hands to scratch them.

Alisha went out.

Thomas sat back down and after a few moments, as usual, the itch started to fade.

He saw that the woman on the other side of the waiting room was peering out the window, watching Alisha yelling at the boys.

'My sister's just asking those boys to move because they're affecting her phone reception,' said Thomas. 'It's my fault, I made this appointment at a really bad time. Alisha always has a big backlog of texting to do after school.'

6

The woman pretended to be reading a magazine.

Thomas waited for yet another itch attack to fade, then took his arm bandage off. No point keeping it on now. He didn't want the doctor distracted from his nipples.

He stuffed the bandage into his pocket and sucked the jam off his arm. When he'd finished he realised the woman was looking at him again and had gone a bit pale.

'It's OK,' he said. 'Jam's good for stab wounds.'

It was a lie, but the woman seemed relieved by the explanation.

Thomas's nipples weren't relieved by the explanation. They started itching again. Thomas couldn't believe it. This was the fourth attack in the last five minutes. He'd never had so many this close together.

He clenched his teeth and waited until the woman was distracted again by Alisha chasing Rocco Fusilli across the medical-centre car park. Then he had a quick scratch and tried to feel if he was growing bosoms. He didn't seem to be, but you could never be sure when it came to medical problems involving puberty.

A gruff male voice broke into his anxious thoughts.

'Thomas Gulliver.'

Thomas dropped his hands guiltily from his chest. The doctor was standing in the doorway of the surgery, beckoning to him.

Thomas stood up.

The moment had come. The moment he'd been dreading since he first began to suspect something awful and scary was happening to him, round about attack twenty-three.

Thomas hoped the doctor had warm hands.

2

'Itchy nipples?' said the doctor, frowning. 'What exactly do you mean by itchy nipples?'

Thomas tried to think how to say it using simpler words.

He couldn't.

'My nipples,' he said. 'They keep getting itchy.'

Dr Ling stood up behind his desk, removed his jacket, rolled up his sleeves and breathed on his fingers.

'Take your t-shirt off,' he said.

Thomas took his t-shirt off.

'How often does this itchiness happen?' asked the doctor.

'Lots,' said Thomas.

Suddenly he was feeling even more anxious than when he walked in. Doctors didn't actually operate in their surgeries, did they?

'How many times a day?' asked the doctor.

Thomas decided to tell the truth, even though

it might result in him being rushed to hospital and given a nipple transplant.

'About ten,' he said. 'Or more.'

'Hmmm,' said the doctor.

Thomas felt encouraged.

Dr Ling wasn't ringing for an ambulance, or sterilizing any scalpels, or backing away to the other side of the room.

He peered at Thomas's nipples and prodded them gently with a fingertip.

'Does that hurt?'

'No,' said Thomas.

The doctor's finger was quite warm, which was a relief. And the doctor wasn't killing himself with laughter either, which was also a relief.

'How long has all this been going on?'

'Two weeks,' said Thomas.

He decided not to add 'and one day and nine hours and fifty-three minutes' in case Dr Ling was one of those medical professionals who got stressed by too much information and had affairs, like on *ER*.

'It's probably just growing pains,' said Thomas, desperately hoping the doctor would agree. 'It'll probably go once I've got more important things to think about, like hair in my pants.'

Oops, that might have been too much information.

Dr Ling looked like he was coping.

'Let's take a closer look,' he said.

He picked up a small metal cylinder from his desk. Thomas saw it was a type of medical torch with a magnifying glass at one end.

Dr Ling switched it on and shone it onto Thomas's nipples.

Thomas was tempted to say 'don't bother' because he'd spent hours in the bathroom in front of the mirror with Dad's car torch. He hadn't seen a single medical problem with either nipple, not even after he'd given them both a really good wash.

But he kept quiet because Dr Ling was a trained professional and Mum always reckoned you should respect trained professionals. She was one herself and if people didn't respect her at the beauty salon they sometimes found themselves having a very painful leg wax.

'Healthy-looking areolae,' said Dr Ling.

'Thanks,' said Thomas.

He hoped healthy-looking was normal.

'They don't seem dry or swollen or inflamed,' said Dr Ling. 'Are your nipples itchy at the moment?'

'No,' said Thomas.

He held his breath and tried to make them itchy. It didn't work. He knew it wouldn't. He had no control over them at all. These days they were like the Zambian wart bugs he'd read about in the *National Geographic* magazine in the waiting room. Foreign and mysterious and scary.

'Do any other parts of your body get itchy?' asked Dr Ling.

Thomas thought about this.

'No,' he said. 'Not like my nipples.'

'Have you been using a different kind of soap?' asked the doctor. 'Or a different washing powder on your clothes?'

'I don't think so,' said Thomas.

Dr Ling switched off the torch and sat down at his desk.

'Well, young man,' he said. 'You've got me baffled.'

Thomas was shocked. He'd never heard a trained professional say that before, not on *ER* or in Mum's beauty salon.

'Here's what I think might be happening,' said the doctor.

Please, begged Thomas silently. Please don't say I'm turning into a girl.

'I think,' said Dr Ling, 'you're experiencing some normal hormonal changes, and possibly a bit of stress. Can you think of anything that might be stressing you?'

'Only my itchy nipples,' said Thomas.

Dr Ling nodded thoughtfully.

'Can I borrow your nipple torch?' said Thomas. 'So I can keep an eye on my nipples at home. Just in case.'

Dr Ling didn't seem to know what to say. He looked at Thomas uncomfortably, a bit like the woman in the waiting room had.

'You don't need to be worrying about that,' said

Dr Ling. 'Anyway, it's my, um, only one and I need it here in the surgery.'

Thomas understood. It was probably a very expensive piece of medical equipment. Dr Ling wouldn't like the idea of it being in a house where teenage boys often visited and stuck things up their noses to try and impress Alisha.

Which was why Dr Ling had just lied.

Thomas stared at the other identical nipple torch on the shelf behind Dr Ling's head. He wondered if he should tell Dr Ling that he understood, so Dr Ling wouldn't feel bad later on about not telling the truth.

Suddenly Thomas stopped wondering and clutched his chest.

'It's happened again,' said Thomas. 'My nipples have gone itchy.'

Dr Ling grabbed the torch and peered at Thomas's chest. To Thomas's relief and slight disappointment he still didn't ring for an ambulance. He didn't even give Thomas an x-ray or an ultrasound.

All he did was take Thomas's temperature, check Thomas's blood pressure and ask Thomas to put his t-shirt back on.

They both sat down.

'I think your condition is almost certainly caused by stress,' said Dr Ling. 'Here's what I think you should do. Each time your nipples get itchy from now on, I want you to have a think about what's happening in your life at that moment, OK?'

'OK,' said Thomas.

'And if the itching doesn't stop, come and see me in a week or two.'

As Dr Ling steered him towards the surgery door, Thomas started thinking back over his most recent attacks and what had been going on in his life at the time.

Dr Ling telling him there was only one nipple torch.

Him telling the woman in the waiting room that jam was good for stab wounds.

Alisha not being honest about her mobile reception.

Him lying about his fake fruit-knife injury.

Thomas stopped halfway out of the surgery door, puzzled.

Could it be?

Was it possible?

He could see Alisha waiting for him, drumming her fingernails and staring at the waiting-room TV. He could feel Dr Ling still trying to steer him out of the surgery.

Should I say something? wondered Thomas. Should I mention the weird possibility that my itchy nipples might have some spooky connection with people telling lies?

He tried to imagine what Dr Ling and Alisha would say.

Alisha would probably roll around on the floor laughing. Dr Ling would probably grab a scalpel and give him a brain examination.

And they'd be right.

Because suddenly Thomas could see what had just given him such a crazy idea.

'I'm a celebrity hairdresser,' said a bald bloke on the screen of the waiting-room TV.

It was *Liar Liar*, the game show where contestants had to guess if people were telling lies.

Thomas felt his chest go itchy.

This time at least he knew why.

His nipples were embarrassed he'd had such a dumb idea.

3

The moment Thomas and Alisha arrived home from the doctor's, things got stressful.

Mum was in the bathroom putting on make-up.

'At last,' she said with a frown. 'We're late as it is, without you two going walkabout.'

Thomas saw that Mum had spotted them in the mirror. He retreated up the hallway and gave Alisha a puzzled look.

Why were Mum and Dad home from work so early? Why was Mum wearing her best jeans and painting her eye wrinkles at five o'clock in the afternoon?

'We're leaving in fifteen minutes,' shouted Dad from the bedroom. 'Who's wrapping Nan's present?'

Thomas's guts went tight.

Of course.

Nan's birthday dinner.

'Sorry,' said Thomas. 'We forgot.'

'I had a year ten refugee and asylum seeker

support group meeting,' said Alisha. 'And Thomas volunteered to stay behind to help pick up litter on his school football pitch.'

It was the story they'd agreed on, but Thomas could see in Mum's mirror that she didn't believe a word of it.

'Is that right?' said Mum as she did some detailed brushwork around her eyes. 'So it was the jam pixies who popped in after school and left the kitchen bench all sticky, was it?'

Thomas felt very foolish and even more stressed. He scratched his itching nipples behind his schoolbag.

Alisha was glaring at him.

Idiot, her look was saying. You'll never be a good liar if you don't remember to clean up the kitchen.

Thomas sighed.

Alisha was an expert liar and she hated being held back by amateurs. This was going to cost him a lot of jelly snakes.

'Don't be cross with Alisha,' Thomas said to Mum. 'She was lying for me.'

Mum gave a big sigh and slowly shook her head. Thomas wasn't sure if it was exasperation or to dry her make-up.

'Get changed, both of you,' she said. 'We'll talk about it in the car.'

Thomas plodded into his room, thinking about the embarrassing confession he would soon have to make to Mum and Dad.

17

Best get it over with in the car, so other people wouldn't hear. It was bad enough being laughed at by the kids at school for having weird nipples. The thought of being laughed at by a restaurant full of strangers made Thomas feel ill.

He flopped down on his bed.

At least telling Mum and Dad wouldn't be so bad now he knew he definitely wasn't turning into a girl. Now he knew for sure what was affecting his nipples.

It was definitely stress.

Once they were all in the car and on their way to pick Nan up, Thomas got even more stressed.

'Love,' said Mum, turning round and looking at Thomas, concerned. 'If you're worried about your nipples, why didn't you say something?'

'That's right, mate,' said Dad. 'Better than lying.'

Thomas stared at them, amazed.

How did they know?

No way would Alisha have blabbed, she just wasn't that type of sister, not even when she was cross with him.

'Doctor Ling rang just before you got home,' said Mum. 'He wanted to let us know that your itchy chest is just from stress and it's absolutely nothing to worry about.'

Thomas braced himself for the itchy-nipple jokes that would now probably come at him from three directions at once.

But Mum just kept looking at him, still concerned.

'Why didn't you tell us, love?' she said.

'Um . . .' said Thomas.

The car started coughing and lurching. Dad revved the engine and swore at it.

All the noise and jolting was making it hard for Thomas to think what to say. Plus the idea of him ever turning into a girl suddenly felt a bit dumb.

Alisha leaned towards the front seats.

'Planet Earth to parents everywhere,' she said loudly. 'Eleven-year-old boys get embarrassed about things like nipples. Der.'

She went back to her texting.

Thomas gave Alisha a grateful look. Even though he was pretty sure the builders in the truck next to them had heard every word.

'Everybody gets embarrassed sometimes,' said Mum to Thomas. 'It's natural. But you can always talk to us, love.'

'We're your parents,' said Dad as the engine spluttered again. 'Mongrel car.'

Mum reached back and patted Thomas on the arm.

'I know me and Dad are very busy,' she said. 'But we're always happy to listen. Why's your arm sticky?'

Thomas wasn't sure if Mum would be happy to hear what he'd done with her favourite jam. Before he could say anything, she reached over further and gently cupped his cheek in her hand.

'We love you, Thomas,' she said. 'And we're all going to help you relax more.'

Thomas could see she meant it.

If he wasn't in a seatbelt, he would have given her a hug.

'Thanks, Mum,' he said.

Alisha let out a squeal of delight.

'Fantastic,' she said, reading her phone. 'Garth's getting a new tattoo. On his back. It says, Store Other Side Up.'

Mum closed her eyes and took a deep breath.

'OK,' she said to Thomas and Alisha. 'Let's please remember that Nan is eighty-three today and she has a very weak heart. It's still only four months since her heart surgery. So we won't tell her anything at dinner that's going to worry or upset her. Nothing about boyfriends or tattoos or stress or nipples, OK?'

'OK,' muttered Alisha.

'OK,' said Thomas.

'Or anything about this mongrel of a car,' said Dad.

'OK,' muttered Alisha.

'OK,' said Thomas.

As they chugged and jolted their way through the traffic towards the old people's home, Thomas glowed inside with love for Mum and Dad.

How many people in the world, he said to

himself, would be this caring and kind? Thinking about a parent's feelings like this. Going to these lengths not to stress or upset a parent.

Suddenly Thomas felt glad he hadn't told Mum and Dad about the kids at school laughing at him. It would only stress and upset them, which wouldn't be fair. They deserved some kindness too.

I'm going to give Mum and Dad the same care and consideration they give Nan, Thomas decided.

This was good.

He was feeling less stressed already.

Except for one worrying thought.

If it was stress that was making his nipples itch, how come he didn't have a nipple attack a few minutes ago during one of the most stressful moments of his whole day?

4

For the first ten minutes of Nan's birthday dinner, Thomas didn't have a single itchy nipple. Not when he and the others trooped into the restaurant, not when they were shown to a table, not when they were given menus.

Thomas's nipples behaved themselves right up until Nan turned to him with a loving smile.

'So, Thomas,' said Nan. 'How are you?'

Thomas hesitated.

Across the table he could see Mum and Dad looking nervous, silently instructing him not to give Nan a heart attack or order anything too expensive from the menu.

'Fine, thanks, Nan,' said Thomas.

Almost immediately his nipples exploded into a massive itch.

Don't scratch them, Thomas told himself.

Keep smiling.

He just managed to. Instead of doing what he

desperately wanted to do. Run through the crowded restaurant. Tear off his best t-shirt. Fling himself into the restaurant kitchen. Relieve his nipples with a cheese grater.

Phew, the itch was fading.

'And how are you, Alisha?' said Nan. 'Doing well at school?'

'Very well, thanks, Nan,' said Alisha. 'I came top in year ten science. Ninety-nine point nine nine per cent.'

Thomas winced even before his nipples went into more itchy spasms. That was a big lie, even for Alisha. He could see Mum and Dad wincing too, wishing Alisha wouldn't be quite so kind and considerate about Nan's feelings.

'I'd have got a hundred per cent,' continued Alisha, 'if I hadn't texted Garth during the exam.'

'Garth?' asked Nan. 'Who's Garth?'

There was a long silence filled only by the clattering and chattering from the other tables.

'Um . . .' said Alisha. 'My dog.'

'Let's look at our menus,' said Dad hastily.

Good idea, thought Thomas.

Except he couldn't even pick his up. Not while he was sitting on his hands waiting for yet another double-strength itch attack to fade.

Thomas stared at the garlic prawns hissing in little oven bowls on the next table. He saw how bulging the prawns' eyeballs were. They looked like they were desperate for a good scratch too.

Thomas's nipples finally calmed down.

Nan looked up from her menu.

'And how about you, Brian and Shirley?' she said to Mum and Dad. 'How's work?'

'Good,' said Mum.

'Good,' said Dad.

Thomas felt his nipples go garlic prawn again.

He knew Mum and Dad weren't telling the truth. Every day when they got home from work, he saw how unhappy and stressed they were. They tried to put on a brave face, but Thomas could tell they were faking it by the way they were always dropping fish fingers and burning peas.

Now he knew exactly how the peas felt.

Arghhh, he screamed, grabbing two glasses of iced water from the next table and plunging his nipples into them.

In his imagination.

But even as Thomas imagined the blissful relief, he knew he was just trying to get his mind off something else.

It was happening again. The spooky thing he'd first noticed at the doctor's.

Each nipple attack was coming immediately after he or Alisha or Mum or Dad said something that wasn't true.

Could this be possible?

Could lies be making his nipples itch?

Thomas wondered if he was going strange in the head as well as strange in the nipples.

'Ready to order?'

The waiter was standing next to the table, his notepad out.

'Has the veal been frozen?' asked Nan. 'Frozen food's dangerous for my health.'

'It's as fresh as you are, gorgeous lady,' said the waiter. 'Fresher.'

Thomas couldn't bear it.

His nipples weren't just itchy again, they were in a frenzy. Did this mean the waiter had lied?

'I'll have what Dad's having,' said Thomas.

He couldn't think about the menu now. He had something much more important to do.

Find out once and for all whether there really was something spooky behind his nipple attacks.

And for that he needed evidence.

Getting into the restaurant kitchen was easier than Thomas had thought.

He didn't have to disguise himself as a waiter or a chef or a piece of crumbed veal.

He simply peeped out of the toilet and waited until both waiters were up the front of the restaurant and both chefs were down the back of the kitchen. Then he crept along behind the cash register and in through the kitchen door.

Thomas crouched behind several big cans of cooking oil and peered through the smoke and steam.

The two chefs had their backs to him. One was

frying something and the other was chopping something with a meat cleaver.

Thomas looked around for a freezer.

He saw a big upright one next to a row of microwave ovens.

As quietly as he could, Thomas crawled over to the freezer. He reached up and pulled the freezer door open. The shelves were stacked with boxes made of waxed cardboard. Printed on some of the boxes were the words *Crumbed Veal 24 Pieces*.

Thomas opened the end of one box as quietly as he could. He peered inside.

Yes.

Veal.

Frozen.

Thomas gave a small shiver.

The waiter had lied. And Thomas's nipples had gone itchy, just like they'd gone itchy with Mum's and Dad's and Alisha's and the doctor's lies.

Thomas struggled to take this in.

His nipples were lie-detectors.

Incredible.

Scary.

The veal wasn't impressed. Twenty-four pieces slid out of the box and clattered onto the floor all around Thomas. They didn't do it as quietly as they could.

'Hey, what's going on?' roared a voice.

One of the chefs grabbed Thomas and dragged him to his feet.

'What do you think you're doing?' demanded the chef.

Thomas tried not to panic. He tried to choose his words carefully.

The chef had a red face and big white bushy eyebrows and was still holding a meat cleaver. Thomas had never been in this exact situation before, but he was pretty sure that a red face and any sort of chopping equipment was not a good combination.

He decided to tell the truth.

'I'm trying to stop you poisoning an old lady with frozen veal,' he said. 'She's got a weak heart.'

As soon as the words were out, Thomas wished he'd chosen them a bit more carefully.

The chef's face was going even redder.

But instead of attacking Thomas with the meat cleaver, the chef gave a big sigh and his whole body sagged.

'Did the waiter tell you the veal isn't frozen?' he asked.

Thomas nodded.

'The waiter with the moustache?' asked the chef.

Thomas nodded again.

The other chef, a younger bloke with a ponytail, let out a groan.

'If Angelo keeps doing that,' he said, 'I'm gunna quit.'

Both the chefs looked so miserable that Thomas felt awful for dobbing.

He was about to apologise when a shadow fell over him and a large hand gripped his shoulder.

Thomas looked up.

The waiter with the moustache was glaring down at him.

The waiter didn't let go of Thomas's shoulder until he'd finished listening to Thomas's explanation and marched Thomas back to the table and pushed him down into the chair.

'Please control your child and his itchy nipples,' he said to Mum and Dad, and went back to the kitchen.

'Busted,' muttered Alisha.

'Itchy nipples?' said Nan to Thomas, concerned. 'Have you got itchy nipples?'

Thomas nodded guiltily, not looking at Mum and Dad.

'It's just a bit of stress,' said Mum. 'The doctor says it's nothing to worry about.'

Nan frowned.

'My grandfather's brother Aaron had something like that,' she said. 'It wasn't nipples, it was . . . what was it . . . teeth, I think. His teeth used to get itchy for no reason.'

Thomas stared at her.

'Or was it his dog's teeth?' said Nan.

Thomas reminded himself that Nan was eighty-three and her memory was almost as clapped-out as Mum and Dad's car.

The meals arrived.

Thomas remembered something himself.

'You mustn't eat that veal, Nan,' he whispered after the waiter had gone. 'It's been frozen.'

'Doesn't matter,' said Nan, chomping happily. 'I like frozen stuff. I just say I don't to keep them on their toes.'

Great, thought Thomas. Nan was lying too. No wonder my nipples were going ballistic.

He had another thought, an awful one.

Was this how he was going to have to spend the rest of his life? Grabbing two glasses of iced water every time somebody didn't tell the truth?

Thomas peered at the garlic prawns he and Dad were having. The prawns didn't look like they wanted to scratch their nipples any more. They just looked sort of worried.

Worried about what was happening to them.

Thomas knew exactly how they felt.

5

Thomas stared in horror at the bosom on the computer screen.

He clicked to make it go away.

It didn't. It stayed there, a lady's bosom, big and pink with a big dark-pink nipple.

Thomas frantically clicked again.

The bosom didn't budge.

'Please,' begged Thomas. 'Go away.'

The nipple on the screen stared at him accusingly. Thomas realised it was sending him a message.

You're very silly, it was saying. Only a silly person would do lie-detector nipple research on this clunky old school computer. You know it's always breaking down. Now you're going to get sprung and you'll be an even bigger joke around here.

'Thomas Gulliver,' said a girl's voice from the other side of the library. 'Do you have a pass to use that computer?'

Thomas froze.

Where had that library monitor come from?

Hastily he propped his folder in front of the computer screen and turned towards the voice.

And saw, with a sinking heart, who it was.

Holly Maxwell, the best behaved and least popular and most dobbing kid in the whole year.

'Well, Thomas,' said Holly. 'Do you have a pass?'

'Yes,' mumbled Thomas. 'But I left it in my bag.'

He tried not to wince as his nipples went itchy.

While he was waiting for them to calm down, another figure leaped out from behind a shelf of books.

Oh no, thought Thomas. Not him as well.

It was Kevin Abbot. The biggest liar and exaggerator in the whole school.

'I've been observing this suspect with my secret undercover skills,' said Kevin to Holly. 'Writing down his criminal activity in my mission log. You know, the twitching and sweating and other stuff people do when they haven't got a library pass.' He held up a battered exercise book. 'I haven't written anything, so I reckon he's telling the truth.'

Thomas stared at Kevin in surprise.

Holly gave Kevin a look too. A brief one of pity and contempt. Then she turned back to Thomas.

'Miss Pearson insists that everyone who uses a computer at lunchtime has to have a library pass,' she said. 'It's to stop kids sneaking in and trying to look at rude websites.'

'I know,' mumbled Thomas.

Behind his back he was giving the mouse lots more clicks, desperately trying to make the bosom on the screen vanish.

'My dad's a law-enforcement officer,' said Kevin. 'He reckons the whole global rude-website industry would collapse if it wasn't for year six boys on school computers.'

Thomas ignored him and kept clicking.

'You're not trying to look at rude websites are you, Thomas Gulliver?' said Holly, coming closer.

'No,' said Thomas weakly.

He could tell she didn't believe him. Her eyes had gone narrow. Her lips were tight. Even her short dark curly hair looked like it didn't believe him.

Thomas wished he could tell her the truth. That he was just trying to find out about lies and nipples. That all he'd found so far was stuff about girls choosing their first bra and women breastfeeding their babies and health advice for pig farmers.

But he didn't dare.

The whole school was already laughing at him. This would give them even more to laugh at.

Through the library window, Thomas could see Rocco Fusilli and the other boys out on the football pitch. Two weeks ago he was out there with them, carefree and happy.

He wished he was there now. Just a normal kid playing soccer. Instead of a freak with lie-detector nipples.

'I'm not looking at rude stuff,' Thomas said to Holly. He clicked some more behind his back and tried to ignore the itch attack that was tormenting him. 'I'm doing research.'

'He is,' said Kevin. 'Nipple research. I saw him.'

Thomas gave Kevin a glare.

'I'm only trying to help,' muttered Kevin, giving Thomas a glare back.

Holly reached forward and snatched the folder away and peered at the computer screen.

Thomas didn't even turn round to look. He just sagged and felt his face getting hot. With these two dobbers on the case, news of his bosom-peeping would be round the school in about three minutes. He could already see the laughing faces and hear the taunts about him buying bras on the Internet.

'Thomas Gulliver,' said Holly. 'I didn't know you were interested in engineering.'

Thomas stared at her.

He turned to the computer.

And stared some more.

On the screen was a display of small weird-shaped metal objects. At the top of the screen were the words *Universal Engineering Supplies – Our Complete Range Of Grease Nipples*.

Thomas pulled himself together.

'Er . . . that's right,' he said, hurriedly reading from the screen. 'I'm particularly interested in the, er, hydraulic zinc-plated button-head concave type of, um, grease nipple.'

Kevin was staring at him, open-mouthed.

Holly wasn't quite so impressed.

More sort of amused, Thomas saw, as he felt his own nipples go hydraulic and button-head. For a fleeting moment he even thought he saw a bit of sympathy on her face.

'Thomas,' said Holly quietly. 'Here's some advice. If a person's worried about turning into a girl, they should probably be researching human nipples instead of mechanical ones.'

Thomas blushed.

But, he saw, there was definitely a bit of sympathy. Her hair definitely looked sympathetic.

Before Thomas could explain that he wasn't turning into a girl any more, Holly grabbed Kevin and dragged him after her out of the library.

Thomas waited until his chest and face calmed down. Then he switched off the computer, made sure nobody was watching, and hurried out of the library too.

What I need, he thought shakily, is a more private type of research.

It wasn't easy, staring at your own nipples through a magnifying glass.

Thomas had to grab handfuls of his chest and make sort of mini-bosoms to see each nipple properly. Which was pretty uncomfortable because he didn't have that much chest to grab. Plus the light bulb in the boys' changing room was so dull he had to hunch forward and squint.

Even so, the nature-excursion magnifying glass from the science cupboard was pretty powerful and Thomas could see more nipple detail than in the bathroom mirror at home.

His nipples didn't look spooky, they looked normal.

Sticky-up bits normal.

Flat bits normal.

The left one, noted Thomas, does look a bit darker than the right one, but that could just be the light in here.

He was tempted to go outside in the sun for better visibility. He decided not to. The rest of the kids were doing gym, and sometimes in the middle of a class Mr Demos the gym teacher popped out for a smoke.

Hunching over even more, Thomas grabbed a fresh handful of chest and pulled it even closer to the magnifying glass.

'What are you doing?'

Thomas spun round.

A kid in gym clothes was standing in the doorway with a handful of tissues pressed to his face.

Thomas recognised him.

Why, thought Thomas despairingly. Why, of all the people to be sprung by twice in one day, does it have to be Kevin Big-Mouth Abbot?

He peered more closely at Kevin's tissues, which were stained red.

Was that jam?

Kevin gingerly pulled the tissues away from his face. Blood dripped from his nose.

'Rocco Fusilli bounced a basketball on my face,' he said. 'Mr Demos told me to run my nose under a cold tap.'

Thomas saw that Kevin was staring again. At the magnifying glass and the bunch of chest Thomas was still holding.

'What are you doing?' said Kevin.

Thomas hurriedly let go of his chest. He glanced at the magnifying glass as if it was a thing of no great interest.

'Science experiment,' he said.

His nipples exploded into itchiness.

Despite feeling embarrassed, Thomas couldn't let this opportunity go to waste. He turned his back to Kevin and examined both nipples through the magnifying glass.

Nothing.

His nipples felt like they were being tickled by a million ants wearing fluffy slippers, but they looked as normal as they usually did.

'Are you ill?' asked Kevin.

Thomas hesitated while the itching faded.

It was a question he'd asked himself a million times.

'You don't have to be embarrassed,' said Kevin. 'My dad's in law-enforcement and he's met people with really weird and gross illnesses. Nothing shocks me.'

Thomas knew what Kevin really meant by 'weird and gross illnesses'.

People turning into girls.

Thomas turned back to Kevin, expecting to see smirking. But Kevin's face had nothing on it but concern and blood.

Thomas was touched.

Here was Kevin, nose a disaster area, concerned about somebody else who wasn't even bleeding.

Suddenly Thomas was tempted to tell Kevin about the spooky thing that was happening to him. Kevin's dad just might have seen something similar in a back alley or a stolen car.

But it was risky.

Kevin Abbot was the kid in the school most desperate to impress other people with boasting and exaggeration. Telling anything embarrassing to Kevin Abbot was a very big risk.

Thomas pictured Kevin blabbing and Mum and Dad finding out that their son was possibly the only person in the world with lie-detector nipples.

The medical tests. The brain examinations. The expense. The worry.

It could kill Nan.

Then Thomas remembered something. Kevin hadn't dobbed him earlier on for not having a library pass.

'Can you keep a secret?' asked Thomas.

'Yes,' said Kevin indignantly.

Thomas's nipples went seriously itchy. He peered

at them through the magnifying glass.

Still normal.

'Is this something to do with grease nipples?' asked Kevin.

Thomas took a risk.

'No,' he said, pointing to his own nipples. 'These ones. When people tell lies my nipples go itchy. I don't know why. It's like they're lie-detectors.'

Kevin stared.

'Is that true?' he said.

'Yes,' said Thomas.

'Really?' said Kevin.

'Yes,' said Thomas.

He could see Kevin wasn't sure whether to believe him.

'Test me,' said Thomas. 'Tell me some stuff and I'll tell you if you're lying.'

Kevin thought about this.

'OK,' he said. He cleared his throat. 'My mum's got a mole on her bum.'

Thomas felt his nipples go fluffy ant. For a second he thought it might be from the effort of trying not to imagine Kevin's mother's bum. But it wasn't.

'Not true,' he said.

Kevin looked impressed.

'Do another one,' said Thomas.

He hoped it wouldn't involve any more of Kevin's family's body parts.

Kevin thought for a moment.

'OK,' he said. 'My sister Courtney likes eating fish spread and date sandwiches in the bath because she can dip them in the water to soften the dates.'

Thomas waited for his nipples to go even more fluffy ant.

They didn't, the itch started to fade.

'True,' he said, feeling faintly sick.

Kevin stared at Thomas's chest in amazement.

'Wow,' he said. 'Lie-detector nipples.'

'You mustn't tell anyone,' said Thomas. 'Not until I find out why this is happening.'

'Complete information lockdown,' said Kevin.

Thomas relaxed a bit.

'Not a word to anyone,' said Kevin, peering closely at Thomas's nipples. 'Not until we're millionaires.'

Thomas stopped relaxing.

Oh no, he thought. What have I done?

6

Thomas hung around after school until the staff room was empty. Then he crept in and put the magnifying glass back into the science cupboard.

He hurried away down the corridor.

'Thomas.'

Thomas froze.

But it wasn't an after-school-care teacher who leaped out from behind the cardboard Roman chariot from the school play, it was Kevin.

'I've been thinking,' said Kevin. 'Dad told me once about this American cop. He's a human lie-detector. He doesn't use his nipples, he uses his small intestine or something. He's a millionaire now.'

Thomas felt his nipples getting itchy.

'Kevin,' he said as they headed towards the playground, 'I can tell when people are lying, remember?'

Kevin looked blank for a moment, then embarrassed. He started walking quickly and talking quickly too. 'OK, the millionaire bit isn't true, but that dopey cop could be rich if he got himself a manager. So could you. You could be rich and the most popular kid in this whole school.'

Thomas was struggling to keep up, both with the walking and the talking.

'How do you mean?' he said.

Kevin stopped and gave Thomas an impatient look.

'Every kid wants to know when they're being lied to,' he said. 'We get lied to all the time. Grown-ups tell us lollies will rot our guts. Friends tell us our iPods just sort of broke. Parents tell us babies get delivered by birds. Kids want to know the truth, and they'll pay for it.'

'Pay for it?' said Thomas.

'Don't worry about the money details,' said Kevin. 'That's why you've got a manager. Me. Just think popular, and rich.'

Thomas stared at Kevin.

He liked the idea of popular, he liked it a lot. But he wasn't sure about the other part. Should a person with a special power charge money for it?

Thomas tried to remember if Superman had a manager and a scale of fees.

He was pretty sure not.

'There's all sorts of ways we can get rich,' said Kevin. '*Liar Liar*, for example.'

Thomas looked at him.

'That game show on telly,' said Kevin. 'The one

where you have to spot when you're being lied to. They have really big prizes. We can clean up.'

'I know the show,' said Thomas.

He also knew it would be cheating, and fraud, and something that would probably get them both arrested by Kevin's dad. He tried to point this out to Kevin. But Kevin wasn't listening. He was staring across the playground, grinning.

'Look at that,' he said. 'Miss Pearson's busting Rocco Fusilli.'

Thomas saw he was right.

On the other side of the playground, a group of after-school-care kids were being yelled at by Miss Pearson.

Kevin was already hurrying closer. Thomas followed, half curious, half guilty. Mum always reckoned telling-offs should be a private thing and Thomas agreed, except when a teacher was really losing it.

Miss Pearson was really losing it. Some of her hair had come unpinned and her upper arms were pink with anger.

Thomas could see why.

Painted on the library wall in big green letters were the words MISS PEARSON LOVES MR DEMOS. Underneath them, faint from where Rocco Fusilli had been made to scrub them off last week, were the words THOMAS GULLIVER IS A GIRL.

Thomas shuddered at the memory.

'How many times do I have to tell you,' Miss Pearson was yelling. 'I don't mind people expressing their creativity, but this is vandalism.'

'I didn't do it,' said Rocco.

Thomas felt his nipples go itchy.

Should he say something? He decided not to. Dobbing was a pretty big crime in these parts.

'It was her,' said Rocco.

He pointed to a girl at the back of the group. The girl's clothes and hands and short dark hair were splattered with green paint.

Thomas's nipples were itching even more now, and so was his curiosity. Rocco was pointing to Holly Maxwell. If he was lying, which he was, how come Holly had paint all over her?

'Holly Maxwell,' yelled Miss Pearson. 'Is this true?'

'No,' said Holly, glaring at Rocco. 'He threw a paint bomb at me after he'd finished doing the graffiti.'

Thomas felt his itch starting to fade. Holly was telling the truth. Thomas wasn't surprised. Holly Maxwell always told the truth.

'I did not throw a paint bomb,' yelled Rocco.

Thomas's nipples went into spasms.

Rocco wasn't even a good liar. His voice had gone squeaky. And he'd been boasting for days about how he was going to get Holly. Just because last Friday when Miss Pearson forgot to set a project, Holly reminded her.

Miss Pearson was staring doubtfully now at the green paint on Holly's hands and clothes.

'Can anyone else tell me what happened?' she demanded.

The other kids stayed silent.

'We didn't see,' muttered one.

The others agreed.

Thomas knew they were all lying. His nipples were so itchy they felt like they were going to burst through his school shirt and do a dance across the playground.

He wished he was brave enough to speak up. But only superheroes could get away with dobbing, even if it was for truth and justice.

'OK, Holly,' said Miss Pearson grimly. 'Come with me. I'm going to ring your parents.'

Holly slumped miserably. She glared at the other kids, who looked away.

Rocco rolled his shoulders and grinned at the other kids, who still looked away.

Thomas found he was speaking before he had a chance to stop himself.

'Holly's telling the truth,' he said.

Suddenly everyone was looking at him. Holly with surprise. Rocco with fury. Miss Pearson with relief. Kevin with the look of a manager who was losing money.

'Did you see what happened, Thomas?' asked Miss Pearson.

Thomas thought fast. He mustn't look like he

was just trying to get revenge on Rocco. He had to find a way of telling the truth without lying. Best to stick to what his nipples knew to be true.

'Rocco did throw a paint bomb at Holly,' he said.

Miss Pearson looked at Thomas. He could see she was trying to decide whether to trust him.

'It's true,' said Kevin. 'We both saw it.'

Thomas tried not to wince as his nipples went into even bigger spasms.

'You mongrels,' hissed Rocco, and several other things that Thomas couldn't hear because Miss Pearson grabbed Rocco and steered him firmly and swiftly towards the staff room.

Thomas saw the expressions on the other kids' faces.

Uh-oh, he thought. This isn't good.

'He can't help it,' said Kevin to the others. 'It's his nipples. They're lie-detectors.'

Karl Lumby, Rocco's best mate, stepped forward and stood closer to Thomas than a person needed to for normal conversation.

'As if,' he grunted.

'It's true,' said Kevin. 'Test him. We won't charge.'

'Lying dobbers,' growled Karl. 'You should stick to being a girl, Gulliver.'

The other kids muttered their agreement. Thomas watched miserably as they trooped over to the monkey bars, throwing him the sort of looks that he'd only ever seen thrown at Holly and Kevin.

Great, he thought. Now I've got out-of-control nipples and an out-of-control mouth.

'Not the best start,' said Kevin. 'But at least we got some publicity.'

'Thanks,' said a voice.

Thomas turned.

Holly Maxwell was looking at him with a strange expression.

'Did you really see what happened?' she said.

'He didn't have to,' said Kevin.

Holly frowned at Thomas.

'So you lied,' she said.

'No,' protested Thomas. 'I didn't actually see, but I didn't . . .'

'You lied,' said Holly.

Thomas could see how disappointed she was.

'Watch the lips,' said Kevin, pointing to his own mouth. 'He's got bionic nipples.'

Holly gave Kevin a look of disgust. 'At least he's better at lying than you are,' she said, and walked away.

Suddenly Thomas wished he hadn't told Kevin about his nipples. Now the whole world would hear about them. And soon the whole world would be sneering and laughing. Except for Mum and Dad and Nan, who'd be stressed and upset.

There was only one thing to do.

'They'll learn,' Kevin was saying. 'They'll learn that our nipples never lie.'

Thomas turned to him and took a deep breath.

'Actually,' he said, 'my nipples are a lie.'

Kevin stared at him.

Thomas felt awful as well as itchy, but he carried on.

'I made the whole thing up,' he said. 'To see how good you are. As an undercover cop.'

Kevin's mouth was moving, but it took a few moments for sound to come out.

'What . . . what about the test?' he said.

'Luck,' said Thomas.

Kevin thought about this.

'You mongrel,' he said bitterly.

Then he ran after Holly.

'Wait,' he called to her. 'I can help you get cleaned up. I've got some special undercover forensic paint-remover.'

Thomas watched them go.

Oh well, he thought sadly. One good thing about not having any friends, I can scratch my nipples whenever I need to.

7

Thomas sat in the beauty salon storeroom, waiting to talk to a nipple expert. Not just a doctor, someone who really knew nipples.

Please, Gwenda, thought Thomas, hurry up.

Usually on a Saturday morning Gwenda was in and out of the storeroom all the time. So far today she hadn't been in once.

Thomas thought about going out into the salon and speaking to her there. He decided not to. Some conversations were best had in private, specially ones about nipples that were ruining your life.

Finally Gwenda came into the storeroom.

Thomas jumped up and closed the door.

'Gwenda,' he said. 'Have you ever had a client with itchy nipples who was very worried because he didn't know what was causing it?'

Gwenda paused in the middle of reaching for a box of tweezers and thought about this.

Thomas waited, hoping she would say yes. Gwenda did all the waxing of men's chests in the salon and she was an expert with years of experience in the area.

'Not really,' said Gwenda. 'I had one who slammed a nipple in a car door once, but that was more of a bruise than an itch.'

Thomas sighed.

'Thanks anyway,' he said.

Gwenda was peering at the front of his t-shirt, concerned.

'Would you like me to have a look?' she said.

'No thanks,' said Thomas hastily. 'I'm just, you know, curious.'

Gwenda's eyes met his.

'Are you asking for a friend?' she said.

Thomas nodded and wriggled a bit. He hoped she couldn't see the truth. That it wasn't his friend's nipples which were suddenly feeling like they were being spring-cleaned with a feather duster.

'Has your friend been to the doctor?' asked Gwenda.

Thomas nodded.

'Doctors,' said Gwenda with a sympathetic shake of her head. 'They don't know as much as they think they do. What your friend needs is a good moisturiser. Ask your mum to get you one from the chemist. I mean him one.'

She grabbed a pair of tweezers and hurried back out into the salon.

'Thanks,' said Thomas, gloomily sitting back down on a cardboard box.

So much for that idea.

A short while later, Mum stuck her head into the storeroom.

'Friend here to see you,' she said.

Thomas stood up, surprised.

A friend? He didn't have any friends. Not since yesterday afternoon.

Mum gave him a fond smile and went back to Mrs Taylor's legs.

Thomas peered out into the salon, and his eyes went wider than the woman in chair three who was having her eyebrows plucked.

Holly Maxwell?

What was she doing here?

For a second, Thomas thought that perhaps she'd come so that Gwenda, who also did nails, could give her a once-over with the nail-polish remover. But that couldn't be right. Standing there in her jeans and t-shirt, Holly didn't have a speck of green paint left on her.

She must have heard I work here on Saturday mornings and just come for a bit of a laugh, thought Thomas sadly.

He looked around to see if Rocco or any of the others had come too, but they didn't seem to have. Then he saw that the lady in chair two had reached out and was stroking Holly's cheek.

Holly looked shocked.

Thomas understood why.

The lady in chair two was wearing a thick green mask of yoghurt-and-seaweed rejuvenating lotion. She looked like an alien with too much make-up.

'You've got lovely skin,' said the green lady to Holly. 'How do you get it so soft and blemish-free?'

'I'm eleven,' said Holly. 'Plus we don't use commercial skin-products at home. My mum reckons they do more damage than good.'

All the women in the salon frowned at Holly.

The green lady's forehead crinkled.

Thomas knew he had to move fast. If Holly carried on like this, things could turn ugly. Mum had a hot-wax machine that could cause intense pain, he'd seen it happen.

'G'day, Holly,' he said, hurrying towards her. 'Would you like to come out the back?'

He turned and headed to the storeroom, hoping Holly would follow.

She did.

'Interesting place to work,' she said once they were inside the storeroom and he'd closed the door. 'Do you get to shave legs?'

Thomas felt himself blushing.

But it was too late. She was here now.

He pointed to a big plastic tub of eggplant-essence foot balm.

'I'm putting this organic skin lotion into bottles

for Mum,' he said. 'The customers prefer to buy it in small bottles cause they can't carry a big tub home.'

Thomas showed her how he scooped the lotion out of the tub in a jug and dribbled it into the bottles.

'Why are you wearing rubber gloves?' asked Holly. 'Is that stuff bad for the skin?'

Thomas felt himself blushing again.

'Don't want my hands to go soft,' he muttered.

But Holly wasn't listening. She'd picked up one of the bottles and was studying the label.

'Says here, one hundred per cent Natural Ingredients,' she said. Then she pointed to the lid of the plastic tub. There was tiny printing on it. 'Says here, Hydroxymethyl Glycinate, Phenoxyethanol and Sodium Hydroxide.'

Thomas stared. He hadn't noticed the tiny printing before.

'Bit of a cheat,' said Holly quietly. 'Putting lotion made from chemicals into bottles that say natural ingredients. Do your mum's customers know this is what she does?'

Thomas glared at Holly. She clearly didn't know that Mum was the most honest beauty salon owner on the planet. On all the planets.

'All it means,' he said, 'is that the bottles are made from natural ingredients and the tubs are made from chemicals. That's all.'

That must be it.

Holly didn't look convinced.

Just what you'd expect from the daughter of two journalists, thought Thomas crossly.

'Look,' he said. 'I'm busy. What do you want?'

'To say sorry,' said Holly.

Thomas stared at her, surprised.

'It was unfair of me, walking off yesterday afternoon,' she said. 'I haven't got a clue how you knew Rocco Fusilli was trying to set me up, and you almost spoiled it with that liar Kevin Abbot, but you were kind and brave. Thanks for standing up for me.'

Thomas could feel his anger fading. It felt like when his nipples went back to normal, only nicer.

Holly smiled at him. He'd never seen her smile before, not properly with her eyes. It was the best smile he'd seen in ages.

He filled a bottle with lotion so she wouldn't notice how happy he suddenly felt.

'So,' she said, crinkling her forehead in what Thomas noticed was a much more attractive way than the green lady. 'How did you know?'

'Know what?' said Thomas.

'That I didn't do the graffiti,' said Holly.

Thomas thought about how much easier it would be to lie. To say he'd actually seen Rocco throw the paint bomb. To say Kevin had got it wrong about the lie-detector nipples. To make up a story about how everyone in the Gulliver family had good eyesight and could see things even when they were up the other end of the school.

But he didn't.

'I've got these nipples,' he said quietly. 'They go itchy. They tell me when people are lying.'

For a long time Holly didn't even look at him. She just stared at the lid of the plastic tub, and at the rows of empty organic bottles on the storeroom shelf.

Even before she spoke, Thomas knew he shouldn't have told her.

'Look,' she said finally. 'I know people give you a hard time, calling you a girl. They call me a goody-goody and a dobber. It sucks. But people won't want to be your friend if you tell them dumb stories just to try and impress them. Me included.'

She opened the storeroom door and went out.

Thomas followed, but Holly was going too fast, striding past the salon chairs towards the street.

'I want skin like hers,' said the green lady to Mum as Holly hurried past.

Holly stopped and turned to the green woman.

'I've got pimples,' she said. 'On my back. And a big scab on this knee.'

Then she strode out the door.

'Whew,' said Mum. 'She's a character. I didn't know she was a friend of yours, Thomas.'

'She's in my class,' said Thomas miserably. 'She's not a friend.'

The green lady winked at Mum.

'That's what my Royce reckoned about his girlfriend,' she said.

'Mum,' said Thomas. 'Can I have a word?'

He turned and went back into the storeroom, hoping Mum would follow.

She did.

'What is it, love?' she said once Thomas had closed the door.

Thomas pointed to the foot lotion bottles.

'These labels say natural ingredients,' he said. He pointed to the plastic tub. 'How come the lotion has chemicals in it?'

He knew Mum would have a simple explanation, but he wanted to know in case a customer ever asked.

Mum was looking a bit uncomfortable.

'They're not really chemicals,' she said. 'They're natural ingredients that sound like chemicals.'

Thomas felt his nipples go feather duster.

He couldn't believe it.

Mum had just lied.

He stared at her in shock. And then was even more shocked by what she did next.

Closed her eyes and let her shoulders slump. Sat down on a box and put her head in her hands.

'Mum?' said Thomas. 'What's the matter?'

Mum took Thomas's hands and looked up at him with the gloomiest, weariest expression Thomas had ever seen her have, and he'd seen her have a few.

'I shouldn't have lied to you, love,' she said. 'You're right, that lotion has got chemicals in it.

It's cheaper than the organic stuff and I'm trying to save money. The salon's going through a bad patch. Not enough customers, too many bills, no profits. When we close up this afternoon, I'm going to have to tell Gwenda I can't afford to employ her any more.'

Thomas was stunned.

Gwenda had worked for Mum for years. This was terrible. No wonder Mum hadn't wanted to tell Nan the truth about work.

Mum stood up and gave Thomas a quick hug.

'We'll pull through,' she said. 'I'm going to work harder than I ever have before. In a few months I'll be able to offer Gwenda her job back.'

Thomas's chest felt very strange. He wasn't sure if it was his nipples telling him Gwenda probably wouldn't be getting her job back, or just worry about Mum.

'We'll all have to work harder,' said Mum, nodding towards the tub of chemical foot lotion.

'OK, Mum,' said Thomas, grabbing an organic bottle.

'Oh, and love,' said Mum. 'Don't say anything about this to Dad. He's got his own worries at work. No point making him feel worse.'

'OK,' said Thomas.

Mum blew him a sad kiss and went back into the salon.

Thomas slumped down on the box.

Poor Mum, he thought.

He was so glad he hadn't burdened her with his mystery nipple illness. Blabbing about the foot lotion had been bad enough.

Thomas sighed.

He wished he had someone he could talk to about all this stuff. Someone who didn't have big problems of their own or a weak heart and wouldn't get too stressed or die.

Not just a nipple expert, someone wise and experienced in solving the complicated problems of the world.

8

Alisha was sprawled on the couch in her bathrobe, reading a magazine and chatting on the phone and sticking a fake tattoo onto her shoulder.

'Garth is so not weak,' she was saying. 'He can pick up a supermarket trolley with his teeth.'

Thomas stood next to the couch, hesitating. Partly because he didn't want to interrupt and partly because his nipples had just gone very itchy.

Alisha looked up and saw him.

'Do you mind?' she said. 'This is a private conversation.'

'Sorry,' said Thomas. 'But there's something I need to talk to you about.'

Alisha glared at him.

'It's a bit urgent,' said Thomas.

Alisha sighed. 'I'll call you back,' she said into the phone. She hung up and looked at Thomas crossly. 'Well?'

Thomas decided to try and calm her down first.

'That's a nice tattoo,' he said.

'Poo or get off the pot,' said Alisha, even more crossly.

'Those pink flowers,' stammered Thomas, pointing to the fake tattoo. 'They're very nice. And the words are nice too, the ones that say, Ten Dollars A Kilo.'

Alisha pulled her bathrobe closed and held up the fingers of one hand.

'Five seconds,' she said. 'Four . . . three . . .'

'The salon's going broke,' blurted Thomas. 'And Mum's telling lies about her organic foot lotion.'

He waited while Alisha took this in.

She looked at him doubtfully.

'How do you know?' she said.

'Mum told me,' he said. 'But we mustn't tell Dad.'

Alisha thought about this, chewing her lip. Thomas knew that meant she was concerned. When she was relaxed she just chewed gum.

Then she did something that really surprised Thomas. She swung her legs off the couch and patted the cushion next to her.

'Park your bum,' she said.

Now Thomas knew she was really concerned. She hadn't invited him to sit next to her for about eight years.

'Did Mum actually tell you the salon's going broke?' said Alisha.

'She didn't actually say broke,' admitted Thomas. 'She said bad patch.'

Alisha did something else that surprised Thomas. She put her arm round his shoulders and gave him a hug.

Just a quick one.

'You are a cretin,' she said. 'Worrying for nothing. Mum's really good at the beauty game. The customers love her. All businesses have dodgy patches. I bet it's not as bad as you think.'

Thomas hoped she was right.

'So why is she telling lies about her foot lotion?' he said. 'The customers think it's got eggplant in it and it hasn't.'

'Listen, you idiot,' said Alisha gently. 'Everybody lies. It's how the world is. I tell Garth I've lost weight because I want him to think I'm thin. You tell people you've got stressed nipples because you want them to think you're interesting. We all do it.'

Thomas didn't know how to reply. He tried to think of a nice way of saying 'you're wrong about my nipples'.

He couldn't.

'Not everybody lies,' he said to Alisha. 'There's a girl in my class who hasn't told a lie in her life. And Dad doesn't lie, except to Nan.'

Alisha didn't seem to be listening. She was looking at her magazine again.

'Anyway,' she said. 'If Mum's salon does go broke, it'll be for a reason. Look, Mum's horoscope reckons everything happens for a reason.'

Then Alisha frowned at Thomas as if she'd just thought of something.

'Why did Mum tell you about the salon?' she said. 'She didn't say anything to me.'

'Well . . .' said Thomas.

He took a deep breath.

'She didn't tell me at first,' he said. 'She tried to hide it. But I knew she was lying cause my nipples went itchy.'

Alisha looked at him.

Then she grabbed her mobile and stood up.

'Word of advice from your big sister,' she said. 'This itchy nipple thing, clever idea, but you're pushing it too far.'

Before Thomas could reply, she'd turned away and was heading towards her room, already talking on the phone.

Thomas flopped back onto the couch.

He'd mentioned his chest on purpose. Just in case Alisha knew something about lie-detector nipples. She did read a lot of magazines.

Oh well.

A politician was on the early evening TV news, looking stern and a bit indignant and telling journalists that he definitely didn't know anything about any bribes.

Thomas tried to work out what the politician was talking about. Something about some dictator and some war that started because of wheaties or something. Thomas wasn't very interested in politics, or breakfast cereal, and he wouldn't have been bothered now except his nipples had just gone feather duster.

Looks like Alisha's right about one thing, he thought gloomily. If a very important person like that tells lies, everybody's probably doing it.

Thomas remembered how, when he was little, Mum and Dad had always told him that lying was naughty and wrong and only bad people did it.

Which was also a lie, he now thought sadly.

Then another thought hit him.

What if that horoscope is right? What if everything does happen for a reason? What if I've been given lie-detector nipples for a purpose?

Thomas wondered what the purpose might be.

A career in the police?

Weekend work as an exhibit in a museum?

He couldn't think of anything else. He was finding it hard to concentrate because there was an ad break on TV and a famous soapie star was talking about an insect spray that she and all her kids loved, and his nipples were going itchier than a mozzie bite.

Thomas clicked the TV off and rubbed his chest until his nipples calmed down.

Then suddenly he thought of another possible purpose for lie-detector nipples, one that made his heart beat faster and his hands go sweaty.

What if my itchy nipples aren't an illness or a career skill, he said to himself. What if they're a special power? For a special mission?

Thomas remembered how good he'd felt speaking up for Holly after school. Before she'd called him a liar.

Was this the reason for his nipples?

To help people?

He stared at the blank TV screen, thoughts racing.

There was only one way to find out.

9

Thomas started his mission in McDonald's.

At the table next to his, two little kids were sobbing. They wanted cheeseburgers and their mum had bought them salads.

'Don't cry,' she was saying, dabbing their tears with serviettes. 'You can have cheeseburgers this afternoon.'

Thomas felt his nipples kick into action.

He waited until the mother was at the counter getting more serviettes, then leaned over to the kids, who weren't crying so hard now.

'Don't stop,' he said. 'She's lying.'

The little kids looked at him, terrified.

Both their faces crumpled and they started howling again.

Thomas stayed at his table, licking his soft-serve cone, while the mother tried unsuccessfully to stop their tears. He waited until she gave in and bought two cheeseburgers. Then he stood up, gave the little kids a wink, and headed off to help others in need.

'Nan,' said Thomas as they sipped their tea in the lounge room of the old people's home. 'You know when the matron gives you your pills and tells you you'll feel better if you take them? I think she's telling the truth. In fact I know she is.'

Nan took a bite of biscuit and thought about this for a while.

Thomas watched her closely. It was hard to tell with old people's faces whether they were confused or just chewing.

'Is that right?' said Nan after a bit. 'I'd better take them, then, hadn't I?'

She reached into her bra, found the pills she'd stuffed in there earlier, popped them into her mouth and swigged them down with a gulp of tea.

'Thanks,' she said to Thomas.

'That's OK,' he said.

Mission accomplished.

An elderly man tottering past tried to take Nan's last two biscuits.

Before Thomas could move, Nan's arm shot out and grabbed the old bloke's wrist. She prised the biscuits from between his fingers.

'There's more in the kitchen,' she said to him. 'Don't be lazy.'

As the elderly man headed towards the kitchen, muttering, Thomas wondered if perhaps Nan wasn't quite as fragile as Mum and Dad thought she was.

'How are your nipples?' said Nan.

Thomas looked at her, shocked. How did she know about his nipples? Then he remembered the waiter had mentioned them at her birthday dinner.

'Not too bad,' said Thomas. 'I'm learning to live with them.'

It was the truth.

'Good,' said Nan. 'But you should be careful with itchy nipples. You remember my grandfather's brother Aaron?'

'I think so,' said Thomas.

He vaguely remembered Nan saying something at the dinner about Aaron's teeth.

'Aaron died when he was twelve,' said Nan. 'They never knew what caused it, but they thought it was something to do with his itchy teeth.'

Thomas nearly dropped his tea.

Twelve? That was awful. And scary.

For a few moments he felt so weak he almost asked for one of Nan's pills.

Then he told himself to calm down because Nan was eighty-three and her memory was almost as clapped-out as Dad's car.

After his success helping Nan, Thomas decided to try something a bit more ambitious.

'Mr Demos,' he said. 'Can I ask you a personal question?'

Mr Demos was having a quiet smoke round the back of the gym while his class did push-ups inside. He looked down at Thomas with a weary expression. Thomas was glad he'd chosen a moment when Mr Demos was relaxed.

'Do you love Miss Pearson?' asked Thomas.

Mr Demos had a small coughing fit.

'No,' he said. 'I do not. You of all people, Thomas Gulliver, should know not to believe everything you read on walls.'

'Sorry,' said Thomas. 'I just wanted to be sure.'

'I wish you were that thorough with your soccer practice,' said Mr Demos. 'Now run along.'

Thomas didn't run. He left slowly because of how much his nipples had started itching when Mr Demos said he didn't love Miss Pearson.

In the library, Thomas found the person he was looking for at her computer.

'Miss Pearson,' he said. 'Can I ask you a personal question?'

Walking home from school a few days later, Thomas wondered if he could make a future career out of helping people and whether, as Prime Minister, he'd be allowed to scratch his nipples in public.

He was still wondering about this when Rocco Fusilli jumped out of a hedge and grabbed the front of Thomas's shirt and tried to lift Thomas off the ground.

He wasn't strong enough, but it still hurt.

Thomas could feel shirt cloth cutting into his armpits. He wondered which would pop first, his shirt buttons or his arm sockets.

'It was you, wasn't it?' grunted Rocco through clenched teeth.

'Ggghhh?' gurgled Thomas, gasping for air.

'Don't lie,' said Rocco. 'It was you left those Valentine cards in Mr Demos and Miss Pearson's pigeon holes. And now they're going out together and everyone thinks it was me.'

'Sorry,' croaked Thomas.

To Thomas's relief, Rocco gave up trying to lift him and dropped him back down onto the footpath.

'Miss Pearson keeps giving me things,' panted Rocco accusingly. 'Books. I only read magazines. Books are for girls.'

Nearby, Rocco's mates jeered in agreement.

Thomas was surprised to find his nipples were staying normal.

That's interesting, he thought. They respond to people lying but not people saying dopey things that are totally wrong.

'What about your girlfriend?' he asked Rocco. 'Why don't you ask Debra to read the books to you?'

Rocco looked startled, like someone who'd just been sprung. He glanced guiltily at his mates, muttered something about not wanting to catch girl germs from Thomas, and hurried away.

Thomas felt sore in several places, but also slightly amazed.

That, he thought as he checked his armpits for damage, was probably the first totally truthful conversation I've ever had with Rocco.

When Thomas arrived home, Garth was out the front, crouched down next to the hedge, talking into his mobile.

'I do love you,' he was saying. 'Honest.'

Alisha mustn't be home, thought Thomas. Unless they prefer doing love stuff over the phone.

Garth looked up and saw Thomas and did a nervous twitch.

Thomas decided he'd better make some conversation. It was what younger brothers were expected to do with their older sister's boyfriend.

'She's usually home by now,' Thomas said to Garth. 'Probably won't be long.'

'Yeah, er, I'm talking to Alisha now,' said Garth.

Thomas had a twitch himself.

His nipples were going ants in fluffy slippers.

Garth was lying.

Thomas almost said something, then decided not to. Garth was about twice as big as him, and Alisha reckoned he had a savage temper from too many spicy pizzas.

As Thomas stepped into the house, he heard Alisha in her room. Her door was open a crack and he could see she was on the phone.

'Bull, Natasha,' she was saying. 'Garth so is faithful. I don't care what that slug Bree reckons.

Garth is one hundred and ten per cent faithful.'

Thomas tapped on the door.

Alisha glared at him.

'Go,' she said. 'Away.'

'It's important,' said Thomas. 'Really important.'

'Half a sec,' said Alisha into the phone. 'I just have to kill my little brother.'

She came over to the door, still glaring at Thomas.

'Before I slam the door in your face,' she said, 'tell me what could possibly be so important that you interrupt me when I'm doing my homework with Natasha.'

'Garth's outside,' said Thomas. 'He just told somebody else he loves them.'

Thomas sat on the couch, waiting for his nipples and his ears to stop tingling.

There's no justice, he thought gloomily. I try to tell Alisha the truth and she yells at me for ten minutes, and now she's out the back kissing the bad guy.

Thomas could feel himself going off the whole idea of a mission. His nipples were more of a curse than a special power. First Holly, then Rocco, now Alisha. Any part of your body that could get you into that much trouble had to be a serious medical problem.

'G'day champ,' said Dad, breezing into the living room. 'Mum still at work?'

Thomas nodded. He wasn't really in the mood for cheery chat.

70

'Work, work, work,' said Dad, flopping into an armchair. 'I'm pooped. I have done so many deliveries today.'

Thomas's nipples went feather duster.

He stared at Dad.

Did Dad just lie?

'You have a busy day?' asked Dad.

Thomas nodded again. He waited for his nipples to calm down so he could think straight.

Relax, he said to himself. Dad's just exaggerating a bit. It's what fathers do with their sons. Dad's probably always done it, but I haven't had the nipples to notice it before.

'I had some news today,' said Dad. 'They're giving me a new truck next week.'

Thomas winced as his nipples went double feather duster.

He waited for the itching to get even worse. Which would be happening any second now when Dad started exaggerating about the huge size of his pretend new truck.

Dad was rolling his eyes. 'A smaller one, if you don't mind.'

Thomas's nipples went double feather duster with mozzie bite.

'That's awful,' said Thomas.

Which it was.

Dad wasn't exaggerating, he was lying.

'It won't even have a mobile phone,' said Dad. 'So people won't even be able to ring me at work.'

Thomas winced as another pulsating itch tore through his chest.

Dad went out to the kitchen to make a cup of tea.

Thomas massaged his chest and tried to think why Dad would be lying.

After a while he remembered what Mum had said at the salon, something about Dad having problems at work.

Of course, thought Thomas. Dad's lying out of kindness and consideration. So me and Mum and Alisha won't worry. Which means his work problems must be pretty big.

Thomas remembered Dad telling him once about one of the other drivers who got addicted to pink lemonade and drank part of his delivery each day and ended up with a criminal record and really bad teeth.

Thomas felt sick with worry.

He wished he could ask Dad what was going on. Just have an honest talk and get it all out in the open. Except if Dad wanted to talk about it, he wouldn't be telling lies, would he?

There must be another way to find out.

Thomas could only think of one.

He'd have to do a last mission.

10

Wednesday 8.15 a.m.
Dad up other end of carriage. Lucky train crowded so he can't see me. I can see his work jacket and lunchbox. Other passengers staring at me. First time they've seen this? Kid writing an undercover mission log on beauty salon notepaper? No, kind woman points to my hair. Twigs. From hiding in our hedge waiting for Dad to leave house. Don't tell her this. Or that I'm investigating Dad's work problems.

8.27 a.m.
Something strange going on. Dad didn't get off at his station. I can see soft-drink factory through train window. Trucks being loaded, so there's not a strike or flavouring shortage. We're heading for the city.

9.03 a.m.
City. Dad into café. I pretend to jot down prices of golf equipment in shop window across street. Dad

talking to waitress. Must be arranging future soft-drink deliveries. I can see why he didn't bring truck into city. Traffic terrible. Must be why he's getting a smaller truck. Easier to park.

9.24 a.m.
Dad still in café. Drinking tea and reading paper. Probably waiting for them to fill out order form. Hope they finish it soon. I've jotted down golf equipment prices twice. Golf ball prices three times.

9.43 a.m.
Man walking past tells me golf equipment prices much cheaper in his brother's shop in western suburbs. My nipples go itchy. Alisha right, world a dishonest place. No wonder people get stressed and need eggplant foot moisturisers.

10.15 a.m.
Dad leaves café. Gives waitress money. She doesn't give him anything. Obviously changed her mind about soft-drink delivery. I follow Dad down street. Stay out of sight behind shoppers and tourists. Dad not arranging soft-drink deliveries with any of them.

10.34 a.m.
Long walk across city. Keep almost losing Dad. Too many people. Wish Kevin was here to give me undercover hints. Or Holly to explain how journalists write while they walk. There's Dad. He's going into

*cinema centre. Their soft-drink order must be huge.
Will Dad be able to handle it with small truck?*

10.42 a.m.
Dad buys ticket. Goes into movie. Batman. *Hang on,
I get it. Dad once told me more soft drink consumed
in cinemas than any other place. He must be doing
consumer research. He's always giving his company
ideas for new products. Blue lemonade, etc.*

10.49 a.m.
*Very mysterious. Just remembered cinemas don't need
deliveries of bottles and cans. Got their own machines
that make soft drinks. Maybe Dad trying to persuade
them that cans are better. If you buy several, you can
sit on them to see over person in front.*

12.11 p.m.
*Feeling hungry. And dumb. Forgot to put my lunchbox
into schoolbag.*

12.16 p.m.
*That's lucky. Found part of old cake under sports
socks.*

1.02 p.m.
*Getting a bit worried. Dad just came out of movie at
end of session. Bought another ticket and went straight
into another movie. I can't see which one from behind
this life-size cardboard Batman.*

1.07 p.m.
Checked box-office screening times. Dad watching
Death Wish 4. *About dangers of taking big delivery*
trucks into the city? Ticket seller won't tell me. Says
he can't because it's rated MA15+. Suspicious looks at
my school uniform. Told him I'm here with my father,
who will be out of movie at 2.46.

2.46 p.m.
Very worried. Dad out of movie, bought another
ticket, now he's in Toy Story 3. *What's going on?*
Dad said he'd take me to see Toy Story 3. *Can't think*
straight. Weak with hunger. Buy small popcorn. All I
can afford, only one week's pocket money with me. Sit
on steps to eat and think.

3.01 p.m.
That must be it. Of course. Why didn't I think of it
before? Dad's quit his job to start new career. He's
always going on about how he should replace person
who writes about movies in local paper because that
person an idiot.

Dad knows heaps about movies. Always chooses
Hollywood when we play Trivial Pursuit. Knows title
of every action movie ever made. I think I'm named
after Tom Cruise.

But why is Dad lying about new job? Must be
because he wants to get really good at it before he
breaks news to us. Probably takes a lot of practice,
writing in the dark. You'd have trouble seeing

dictionary if you need to check spelling of Angelina Jolie or Antonio Ba–

'Thomas, what are you doing here?'

Thomas almost dropped his mission log.

He scrambled to his feet, looking around in alarm. Sprung.

Dad was coming down the steps from the upper level of the cinema centre. He was carrying a dripping lunchbox and dabbing at a wet patch on the front of his jacket. And staring at Thomas, amazed.

'You should be in school,' he said.

Thomas was tempted to say 'you should be at work', but he didn't. Perhaps Dad was at work.

'What are you doing here?' said Dad again.

Thomas hesitated. A million excuses ran through his head. Most of them involved lying about being on a school geography excursion to see *Batman*.

He decided to tell the truth.

'I was worried about you,' said Thomas.

Dad looked down at his dripping lunchbox and jacket.

'I spilled my drink,' he said. 'These cardboard drink cups are hopeless.'

Thomas wished he had some tissues or a hair-dryer in his schoolbag. Poor Dad. He looked shocked at being sprung too. Thomas felt like giving him a hug. He didn't.

'Why aren't you at work, Dad?' he said.

He hoped Dad would say 'I am', and be telling the truth.

Dad looked away.

'Day off,' he said.

Thomas's chest burned with itchiness on the outside and ached with disappointment on the inside.

'Then why,' he said softly, 'did you pretend you were going to work this morning?'

Dad looked at Thomas for a long time.

Suddenly he closed his eyes and his shoulders slumped. He sat down on a step and put his head in his hands.

'I was fired three weeks ago,' he said. 'I've been trying to get another job. Nobody wants me.'

Thomas didn't know what to say. He sat down and put his arm round Dad's shoulders.

He felt numb. No wonder Dad had lied.

'Did you follow me all the way here?' said Dad.

Thomas nodded.

Dad looked at him again. For an awful few moments, Thomas thought Dad was going to burst into tears.

But Dad just kissed him on the top of the head.

'You're one in a million, Thomas,' said Dad. 'There aren't many kids like you, you know that, don't you?'

Thomas didn't reply. Dad was right, but no way was he going to make Dad's stress worse by telling him about lie-detector nipples.

Dad was staring down at the carpet.

'Sorry I lied to you, son,' he said.

'That's OK, Dad,' said Thomas.

His chest, which had calmed down, went hot and bothered again.

Dad thought for a moment.

'Best not say anything about this to Mum,' he said. 'She's got her own worries at work. No point making her feel worse.'

Thomas nodded again. He'd sort of been expecting this.

'I'll get another job soon,' said Dad. He frowned for a while, then brightened. 'Hey, do you want to see *Toy Story 3* with me?'

As Thomas walked home with Dad from the station, he tried to think of cheerful things to say about the movie.

But he didn't feel cheerful.

Dad was lost in his own thoughts, and soon Thomas was too, remembering how much better things had been before his nipples started filling his days with sadness and worry.

Why me? he said silently to his nipples.

Thomas remembered how stressed he'd been when they first started going itchy. Sitting in the doctor's waiting room, panicking that he was turning into a girl.

Big deal.

I wish I had turned into a girl, said Thomas

silently to his nipples. I'd rather be a girl any day than have to put up with you two.

He waited for a sign that his nipples were listening.

Nothing.

Not even a tweak.

Now I haven't even got any friends thanks to you, he said to them. And I have to keep secrets from my own parents.

Thomas wished his nipples would shrivel up and drop off. But they didn't. They stayed exactly where they were.

They were still there when Thomas and Dad walked into the kitchen and Mum peered up from her business accounts with a weary frown.

'You're early,' she said to Dad.

'I deserve a bit of time off,' said Dad. 'The deliveries I've made this week.'

Thomas tensed his chest to try and make his nipples less itchy.

It didn't work.

It never did.

Mum turned to Thomas, not frowning quite so much.

'And you're late,' she said. 'There's somebody here to see you.'

11

'Hello, Thomas,' said Holly, getting up from the couch.

Thomas's nipples went garlic prawn.

For a moment, he was confused.

How could 'Hello' be a lie?

Then he realised what had happened. The TV was on. It was a news report about whales being hunted, and a Japanese fisherman was claiming that Japan only kills whales for scientific research.

Thomas gave Holly a nervous grin.

'G'day,' he said.

Whatever she'd come for, he hoped it wouldn't involve talking in a loud voice about him not being at school today.

'Can we talk in private?' said Holly.

Good idea, thought Thomas, and led her into his room.

As he closed the door behind them, he wondered if Holly was going to start accusing him of being a liar and a foot-lotion fraud again.

'I've been thinking about your nipples,' she said.

Thomas tensed.

Already it wasn't sounding good.

'And I've been thinking that I was wrong,' said Holly. 'I reckon if you were a liar you wouldn't have done what you did, dobbed Rocco and made yourself the most unpopular kid in the school. Only a decent and honest person would do that. So I believe you about your nipples. The lie-detector stuff and everything.'

Her eyes were big and sincere and he could see she meant it. Even her short tufts of hair looked sincere.

Thomas felt weak with surprise. And hunger. He'd only had a small popcorn and half an old cake to eat all day.

He flopped into the chair at his desk.

'Thanks,' he said. 'I'm glad you believe me.'

Holly gave him one of her grins, like she had at the salon. Except this one was a bit different. It was just as friendly, but she looked sort of tense at the same time.

'Thomas,' she said. 'I'm afraid I've got some bad news about your nipples.'

He stared at her.

Bad news?

Holly rummaged in her pocket and pulled out a piece of paper.

'Shift over,' she said, and sat down next to him

at his computer.

Thomas prayed Alisha wouldn't come in. As far as Alisha was concerned, sharing a chair with someone meant you were going out with them.

Holly was typing a website address.

'I did some research on the net,' she said. 'About itchy nipples and stuff.'

'So did I,' said Thomas. 'All I could find was information about breastfeeding and pigs.'

'I'm lucky,' said Holly. 'My parents taught me how to use search engines properly. I found this.'

The computer screen was now full of print.

'It's a magazine article,' said Holly. 'From France, from a few years ago. It's about people called doubters.'

'Doubters?' said Thomas.

'I think that's the right word,' said Holly. 'The article was written in French, so I had to download some software to translate it. The software was free but it writes worse sentences than Kevin Abbot.'

'What are doubters?' said Thomas.

'The article reckons they were children,' said Holly. 'They lived at different times in history. Some in France, some in Germany, some in other countries. They all had body bits that went weird when people told lies.'

Thomas stared at her.

Then he turned to the screen and started reading.

Holly was right, the sentences weren't great and

quite a few of the words were a bit dodgy too.

Him nose she burning like a frying, he read. *Him nose of liar. Him nose of truther. Him nose of doubter.*

'This is much worse than Kevin,' said Thomas.

But he kept reading.

Rare and particular had these littles, he read. *Ears she snowing, fingers he wobblement, rump steaks they puffing.*

'It's saying they all had body bits like your nipples,' said Holly. 'Body bits that did strange things when people told lies. Ears that went cold. Fingers that went trembly. Stuff like that.'

Thomas didn't know what to say.

He felt dizzy with relief. He wasn't alone. Other kids had had it too. Maybe he could find out where it came from. How to get rid of it.

'Thanks,' said Thomas, so excited and grateful he grabbed Holly's hands. He realised what he was doing and let go of them quickly.

'The article reckons it's hereditary,' said Holly. 'You get it from your ancestors. But it's only in a few families and it only pops up every few generations.'

Thomas thought about this.

It could explain Nan's great-uncle Aaron's itchy teeth.

'What's the bad news?' asked Thomas. 'You said you had bad news.'

Holly looked at the floor, her face clouding.

'The article says something else about doubters,'

she said quietly. She hesitated and Thomas could see it was something she didn't want to tell him.

'What?' he said.

'They mostly die young,' said Holly.

Thomas felt a curdle of dread in his guts.

'How young?' he said.

'Our age,' she said. 'Eleven or twelve.'

Thomas felt the dread growing. He remembered what Nan had said about itchy-teeth Aaron. How he'd died mysteriously at twelve.

Please, Thomas silently begged his nipples. Go feather duster so I know this isn't true.

They didn't.

Thomas stared helplessly at Holly.

'If I'm a doubter,' he said. 'Does this . . . does this mean . . .?'

He couldn't say the rest of the words. They were too scary.

Holly squeezed his arm. He didn't pull away.

'There is one doubter who didn't die young,' said Holly. 'She's in this article too. A woman called Vera Poulet who lives in France. Her nose used to go hot.'

Holly scrolled down the screen and pointed.

Thomas read more Kevin writing.

Vera Poulet she birth in Boulogne since 1947. Educate in some England. First career working to teach. Housing to Paris since fifteen years past ahead.

Holly scrolled some more. To a photo of a woman with grey hair, dark eyes and a serious face.

Vera Poulet didn't look very friendly and her nose didn't look very hot. But at least she didn't look dead.

'Does it say how she survived?' asked Thomas, reading on frantically.

'Fraid not,' said Holly. 'Sub-editor probably cut that bit out. They're always doing that to my parents' articles.'

'Vera Poulet must know how to survive being a doubter or she'd be dead,' said Thomas. 'I can ask her. Email her. Ring her up.'

'I did,' said Holly.

Thomas wanted to grab Holly's hands again. Nothing romantic, nothing Alisha could make a meal out of, just gratitude.

'Or rather, I tried,' said Holly. 'It says here Vera Poulet works in a place in Paris called the Denfert-Rochereau Catacombs. The translation software reckons that's some sort of pet-grooming business. I've checked lots of internet directories but I haven't been able to find a single place like it in that part of Paris.'

Thomas felt the dread coming back.

'We have to find her,' said Thomas. 'We have to contact her.'

'I know,' said Holly quietly.

Thomas's thoughts were racing. There had to be a way. But if Holly hadn't been able to do it, the daughter of journalists, with all her research skills . . .

An idea hit him.

Before he could say anything, Holly reached out and took his hand.

'We should tell your parents,' she said.

'No,' said Thomas. 'This is a really bad time to be worrying them. Anyway, we don't need to. I've just thought of someone who can help us.'

12

'Are you sure this is a good idea?' said Holly as they hurried towards Kevin's street.

'Definitely,' said Thomas. 'Kevin's dad is in law enforcement. The police are really good at tracking people down. Mr Abbot will know how we can contact this Vera lady in Paris.'

'Aren't you worried he'll tell your parents?' said Holly.

'No,' said Thomas. 'The police have to respect people's privacy. It's the law. Kevin told me once.'

'And when Kevin told you all this,' said Holly, 'had your nipples started their career as lie-detectors?'

Thomas had to admit they hadn't.

'It's still worth a try,' he said.

'You're a very positive thinker,' said Holly. 'That's why I like you.'

Kevin's front yard was very untidy. Thomas wasn't surprised. Miss Pearson reckoned Kevin Abbot didn't know the meaning of the word neat and had probably never even used the word tidy in Scrabble.

The lights were all on in the house, and the curtains and blinds were all open. Thomas and Holly paused at the front gate, trying to see which room Kevin was in.

No sign of him.

All Thomas could see, in the kitchen and the lounge room and the bedrooms, were Kevin's older brothers and sisters playing musical instruments and building models for school projects and making cakes and painting t-shirts and writing essays.

'How many brothers and sisters has Kevin got?' asked Thomas.

'Eight, I think,' said Holly.

Thomas wasn't surprised to hear this.

No wonder Kevin was always getting into trouble for not doing his homework. The noise around here was unbelievable. Somebody was practising the trumpet. Somebody else was using a power tool. About six people were shouting at each other, and it sounded like at least three of them were vacuuming at the same time.

'Psst.'

Thomas jumped.

Somebody was hissing at them from a large bush in the front garden.

'Kevin?' whispered Thomas.

He crept towards the bush.

'You looking for Kevin, love?' said a voice inside the bush.

Thomas peered in. Through the leaves he could just make out two grown-ups. They were sitting on the ground, their backs against the trunk of the bush. Their knees were up under their chins and they were sipping glasses of wine.

Mr and Mrs Abbot.

Thomas stared.

What were Kevin's parents doing hiding in a bush in their own front yard? Surely they weren't on a police operation against their own family?

'Kev's in the garage,' said Mr Abbot.

'Thanks,' said Thomas, feeling awkward. He decided not to say anything about Paris just yet. Best get Kevin to do the actual asking. Plus Thomas wasn't sure if he should be chatting with a police officer who was undercover.

'Are you friends of Kev's?' asked Kevin's mum.

'Um . . .' said Thomas. 'Sort of.'

'We're in his class,' said Holly.

'Poor little bloke,' said Kevin's mum. 'He hasn't got many friends. Don't know why.'

Thomas decided not to say anything. It was like Mum always told him. If you haven't got anything good to say, don't say anything at all.

'You're probably wondering what we're doing here,' said Kevin's mum.

'Not really . . .' said Thomas.

'Hiding,' said Kevin's dad.

'When you've got nine kids,' said Kevin's mum, 'and they're pestering you night and day to look at their projects, sometimes you need a break.'

That seemed reasonable to Thomas.

'I've listened to three versions of *Stairway To Heaven* already tonight,' said Kevin's mum.

'Four,' said Kevin's dad. 'Kevin did one on the xylophone.'

Kevin's mum pulled an exasperated face.

'I'm always doing that,' she said. 'Forgetting Kevin.'

Thomas smiled nervously and wondered how he could get away to the garage. He didn't want to seem rude. Not when the grown-ups he might be upsetting could be armed.

'Don't get us wrong,' said Kevin's mum. 'We're just as proud of Kevin as we are of all the others.'

Thomas kept smiling, even though his nipples were suddenly itching big time.

He wished he hadn't heard Kevin's mum say that.

If only the person in the house who was suddenly playing the drums very loud had started just a few seconds earlier.

Thomas opened the side door of the garage.

He and Holly stepped inside.

'Kevin?' he said.

He peered around in the gloom. A faint haze of street light was coming in around the roller door, but that was it.

'Here's a light switch,' said Holly.

A fluoro strip blinked on.

'G'day, Thomas and Holly.'

Thomas jumped. Kevin was standing in the middle of the garage, completely still, his legs together and his arms sticking straight out at the sides.

Thomas stared, wondering how Kevin could tell who it was when he had a green supermarket bag over his head.

'I could hear your voices,' said Kevin from inside the bag. 'But I couldn't switch the light on cause I'm training.'

'Training?' said Thomas. 'What for?'

Kevin never played sport at school. He was famous for his excuse notes, specially among people who knew he wrote them himself.

'My future career,' said Kevin. 'Undercover cop.'

Thomas and Holly looked at each other.

'When criminals capture you,' Kevin went on, 'this is what they do to you. Make you stand like this for hours till all the blood runs into your feet and your ankles swell and you confess everything. They got the idea from the war on terror.'

Thomas couldn't resist glancing at Kevin's ankles.

They looked as skinny as ever.

'Have you come to say sorry?' said Kevin. 'For lying to me. You sucked me in big time with all that lie-detector nipple stuff. But it's OK, I forgive you.'

Thomas looked at Holly again.

This was going to be the tricky bit.

'I am sorry I lied to you,' Thomas said to Kevin. 'But, um, the nipple stuff is true.'

'It is,' said Holly. 'Thomas is one of a small group of kids throughout history with lie-detector body parts and we're trying to urgently contact a woman in Paris who can save him from dying soon.'

Kevin slowly pulled the bag off his head.

He stood blinking at Thomas and Holly in angry disbelief.

'Rocco Fusilli put you up to this, didn't he?' said Kevin. 'Are you recording this? Well you're in big trouble if you are because recording people for the purposes of bullying is against the law. If I tell my mum and dad about this they'll have both of you watched by satellites.'

Thomas felt his nipples go itchy.

He also felt awful.

'Calm down, Kevin,' said Holly. 'We're not here to bully you.'

'We're not,' said Thomas.

'You mean it's all true?' said Kevin. 'You dying and everything?'

'We need your dad's help,' said Thomas. 'To contact the woman in Paris. We only know she works in a pet-grooming parlour and we thought your dad could help, what with him being involved with law enforcement and stuff.'

Kevin stared at them.

He started fiddling nervously with the green supermarket bag and then seemed to spot something on the garage floor that needed him to stare down at it for a long time.

A horrible feeling started to curdle again in Thomas's guts.

'Kevin,' said Thomas. 'Your dad *is* involved with law-enforcement?'

'Sort of,' said Kevin in a small voice.

Thomas felt his nipples go triple mozzie bite. He also felt his future go bleak. He looked at Holly and saw she was already realising the awful truth.

'Kevin,' said Holly. 'What does your father do?'

Kevin slumped onto an old couch, not looking at Thomas or Holly.

'Car park manager,' said Kevin. 'But he enforces lots of laws. People who park across two parking bays can be prosecuted big time. And there was a blue Toyota on level three last year that was reversing way over the speed limit.'

Holly gave a sigh.

'Sorry we wasted your time, Kevin,' she said.

'Bye, Kevin,' said Thomas.

He felt sorry for Kevin. But he couldn't think of anything else to say. Not when he had so much maths to do. Trying to work out how many months he might have left to live.

'Wait,' said Kevin, jumping up.

Thomas and Holly stopped by the door.

'This woman in France,' said Kevin. 'The one

who can save your life. Why don't you go to Paris and find the pet-grooming parlour and see her in person?'

'Brilliant,' said Holly.

Thomas could feel Holly bristling. He'd never actually seen her do anything violent, but suddenly he had the feeling she could.

'Kevin,' said Thomas. 'I've got about eleven dollars. And my parents have got even bigger financial problems. How can I get to Paris?'

'Your nipples will take you there,' said Kevin.

Thomas saw that Kevin's eyes were shining with excitement. A bit like they had, Thomas remembered, when Kevin had first seen his nipples in action.

'How?' said Thomas.

Despite himself, he felt a small bubble of hope rising inside him.

'I know exactly how,' said Kevin, coming over and putting one arm round Thomas and one round Holly. 'Trust me.'

13

Thomas had never auditioned for a TV show before, and it was a bit scary.

For a start, the crowd was huge.

Thomas peered anxiously around the vast hotel ballroom.

'Relax,' whispered Kevin, massaging Thomas's shoulders. 'Just think of the prize. Not the car, the other one, the overseas trip.'

Thomas tried to relax, but it wasn't easy. A couple of nights ago when he watched *Liar Liar* with Kevin there were three contestants. He hadn't dreamed there'd be this many people wanting to get on the show.

And they were all adults.

Thomas glanced at Holly. She wasn't looking relaxed either.

'Are you sure you want to do this?' she said to Thomas. 'I can ask my parents to lend you the money to get to Paris. They might not, but I can ask.'

'Thanks,' said Thomas. 'But it's too risky. What if they tell my parents?'

Holly chewed her lip and nodded and Thomas could see she understood.

'Attention, everybody.'

A TV producer with a leather jacket and a clipboard walked onto the stage.

The ballroom started to go quiet.

Thomas knew this was the moment.

'Good luck,' Kevin whispered loudly to him. 'Remember, you've got the nipples.'

Several people standing nearby gave Thomas strange looks. Thomas pretended not to notice. He plunged forward towards the stage.

'Sorry,' he said as he squeezed and wriggled between the groups of people. 'I'm looking for my parents.'

Lying was surprisingly easy once you put your mind to it. Once you had a really important reason for doing it. Once it was your only choice.

Thomas wished his nipples felt that way.

He got to the front of the crowd just as the TV producer was starting his speech.

'Welcome to *Liar Liar*,' said the producer. 'Wonderful to see so many of you here. I hope lots of you can be contestants on our show. And I'm not lying about that.'

The crowd laughed.

Thomas didn't because he had to concentrate on what he was going to do next.

'As we told you when you phoned in,' said the producer, 'we'll be auditioning you in groups. But first, just in case any of you are confused and think you're here to audition for *Big Brother*, we're going to start by demonstrating how our show *Liar Liar* works. I'm looking for a volun–'

Before the producer finished saying the word, Thomas scrambled up onto the stage.

A bloke with a walkie-talkie on his belt lunged towards him.

Please, Thomas silently begged the TV producer, please notice I'm a kid.

'Wait,' said the producer to the walkie-talkie bloke.

Thomas tried to look at least a year younger than he actually was. He smiled at the producer with what he hoped was a childish smile. And he saw exactly the look on the producer's face that he'd hoped to see.

Here's a bit of fun, the look said. Some kid thinks he can be a contestant. This'll give us all a laugh. Relax the real contestants. The adult ones.

'What's your name, son?' said the producer.

'Thomas.'

Thomas was tempted to lisp but decided at the last moment that might be overdoing it. Plus he didn't want to risk triggering a nipple attack by faking anything.

'Good on you, Tommo,' said the producer. 'And do you know how our show works?'

Thomas nodded, trying hard not to give the

producer a look which said anything remotely like of course I do you idiot that's why I'm here.

'Good boy,' said the producer. 'Do you want to have a go?'

Thomas nodded again.

The producer started clapping and showed the crowd by raising his hands that he wanted them to clap as well. Most of them did, though Thomas could see that some of them would rather be strangling the pushy kid on stage.

'And now,' said the producer, 'to put Tommo to the test, let's welcome our first Liar Liar.'

More applause.

A bloke about Dad's age came out and stood in the middle of the stage. He was dressed in a parking inspector's uniform.

'I'm a butcher,' announced the man.

Thomas's nipples went itchy and told him exactly what to say.

'Liar,' said Thomas.

Everyone laughed.

Thomas wasn't exactly sure why they were laughing, but it didn't matter. The producer was holding his thumbs up. This was a bit different to the huge flashing electronic wall on the actual show, but it meant the same thing.

Correct answer.

'Last month,' said the man, who Thomas had a feeling was a real parking inspector, 'I went on holiday to Jakarta.'

Thomas frowned. He wanted to look as if he didn't even know where Jakarta was, which he didn't. He also wanted to look as if he was guessing the answer, rather than being told by body parts that had temporarily stopped itching.

'True,' said Thomas.

The producer glanced at his clipboard and put his thumbs up again.

'In Jakarta I stayed near the beach,' said the parking inspector.

'True,' said Thomas.

Thumbs up.

'In a caravan that was double parked,' said the parking inspector.

Everyone laughed. Except Thomas who itched.

'Liar,' he said.

Thumbs up.

'My favourite Indonesian food is *gado gado*,' said the parking inspector.

'Liar,' said Thomas.

Thumbs up.

'I can drink four bottles of Indonesian beer before I need to pee,' said the parking inspector.

'True,' said Thomas.

Thumbs up.

Thomas took some deep breaths to try and calm down.

They won't pick you for the show, he told himself, if you faint with excitement.

Then he saw that the TV producer was giving

him a strange look. And up the back of the ballroom, Kevin was waving to him frantically with lots of throat-cutting gestures.

Thomas felt a jolt of alarm.

In all the excitement he'd forgotten what he'd agreed with Kevin. About not getting a perfect score and making people suspicious.

'On my holiday,' said the parking inspector, 'I met some Indonesian parking inspectors.'

Thomas felt his nipples go itchy. He ignored them.

'True,' he said.

The producer put his thumbs down. The crowd groaned. The producer, Thomas was pleased to see, looked almost relieved.

Then a worrying thing happened. Thomas's nipples went even itchier.

Oh no, thought Thomas. Of course. I just told a lie and my nipples know it.

This was getting complicated.

Please, Thomas silently begged his nipples. Don't confuse me now.

Thomas held up his hands as if he was feeling a bit shaky and anxious and needed a moment to calm down.

Which was true, for him and his nipples.

'Take a deep breath, Tommo,' said the producer. 'You're doing well.'

'Thanks,' said Thomas.

The parking inspector said thirteen more

things about his holiday, including claims that he'd eaten barbecued snake, met Natalie Imbruglia in a shopping centre, had three suits made and given a parking ticket to an illegally parked lobster.

Thomas made sure he gave wrong answers to another three of them. Four mistakes out of twenty seemed about right. Not too suspiciously clever-clogs, but good enough to be picked for the show.

While the crowd was applauding at the end of Thomas's audition, Thomas glanced at the TV producer.

There was a very different look on the producer's face now.

I'm a very happy TV producer, the look said. We haven't had a kid contestant before. This is going to make our show even more popular with young viewers than *Who Wants To Be A Millionaire* or *America's Next Top Model*.

Thomas peered out across the crowd and saw Kevin and Holly. Kevin was grinning and applauding harder than anyone. Holly was looking even unhappier than before.

Suddenly Thomas knew why.

He felt a stab of guilt.

Stop it, Thomas said to himself. It's not cheating when you're doing it to save your own life.

It's not.

14

'It's not cheating,' said Kevin indignantly. 'No way.'

Thomas gave Kevin a look, begging him to be quiet.

The *Liar Liar* hospitality room at the TV studio was crowded with contestants and their families, all trying to calm their nerves before the taping of the show. Most of them were trying to do it by eating noisily at the buffet. But the slurping and chattering wasn't loud enough to drown out Kevin when he was being indignant.

Thomas tried to steer Holly and Kevin away from the crowd.

'No way is it cheating,' Kevin said to Holly, his eyes bulging with indignation and his cheeks bulging with turkey-and-prawn sandwiches. 'It's just Thomas using his talent.'

Although Thomas was grateful for Kevin's support, he was tempted to pop another couple of sandwiches into Kevin's mouth to shut him up.

'I never said it was cheating,' muttered Holly.

'That's right,' whispered Thomas. 'She didn't.'

Since the audition she'd been thinking it, Thomas could tell. But she hadn't said anything, not once. A couple of days ago he'd thanked her for not going on about it.

'You're my friend,' she'd said quietly, her dark eyes meeting his. 'I don't want you to die.'

Thomas hadn't needed his nipples to know she was telling the truth.

'If it's cheating,' said Kevin loudly, reaching for more sandwiches, 'then the Socceroos are cheating when they do good kicks.'

A couple of people turned and looked at Kevin.

Thomas wondered if it would be cruel to stuff celery sticks up Kevin's nostrils so he suffocated.

Holly saved him the trouble.

'Kevin,' she said, holding a small grey object in front of his face. 'If you mention cheating one more time I'll make you eat this oyster.'

Kevin closed his mouth.

Mum and Dad and Alisha came over.

'We think you're very brave,' said Mum, patting Thomas's arm. 'We've been having a little talk, and we think we know why you want to do this.'

'So I can win,' said Thomas.

Sometimes parents, even highly skilled and creative ones, could be a bit slow.

'There are some really good prizes,' added Thomas, to make it crystal clear.

Not too crystal clear, though. Best not break it to Mum and Dad that they were all going to France until he'd actually won.

'You're right, there are some great prizes,' said Dad. 'But, son, the important thing is to do your best. That's much more important than prizes.'

'What he's really saying,' said Alisha, 'is if you don't win the car you're dead.'

'Fingers on buzzers . . .'

The show started with what the compere called a quick fingers round. There were three contestants, and the purpose of this round was to see who would get first choice of the Liar Liars.

Thomas took a deep breath and concentrated on losing.

'My hair . . .' said the compere, and the studio audience exploded with laughter. The compere was famous for his hair transplant. Thomas looked at the famous hair gleaming in the lights and was glad he hadn't had a nipple transplant. He'd hate to have nipples that shiny.

'My hair,' said the compere, 'used to belong to Bert Newton.'

The audience laughed again, and the contestants lunged for their buzzers.

Thomas paused. While the others both buzzed *Liar*, he ignored his itchy chest, then buzzed *True*.

'Oh, Tommy, you kind boy,' said the compere with a theatrical sigh. 'If only you were right. I'd give anything for talented hair. Thank you for your faith in me, but I'm afraid you were slow and wrong and so you go last.'

The audience gave a sympathetic groan.

Thomas managed not to smile.

Perfect.

Now he would know exactly what score he needed to win, and he wouldn't have to get too many right and risk making the producer suspicious.

The contest started.

Thomas won it easily with sixteen out of twenty.

'Congratulations to our youngest ever winner,' said the compere, putting a shiny-jacketed arm around Thomas's shoulders. 'You've won a fully-weatherproof set of garden furniture, plus barbeque. You can either take the prize or come back tomorrow night and compete again.'

'I'll come back tomorrow night,' said Thomas.

He squinted into the lights, trying to see Mum and Dad and Alisha and Holly and Kevin in the audience.

At first he couldn't. The lights were too bright. Then he saw them, over to one side. They were all applauding.

Mum and Dad seemed particularly pleased that tomorrow night he'd be trying for a bigger prize.

Tomorrow night turned out to be later that morning.

'We tape a whole week's episodes in one day,' said a production assistant while Thomas and the two new contestants were having a cup of tea. 'Don't worry, you'll probably be finished by lunchtime.'

Not if I can help it, thought Thomas.

He won the second night with seventeen out of twenty.

'Incredible,' said the compere. 'And I'm not lying. Young man, you've won a holiday for your whole family to the Great Barrier Reef, staying at –'

'I'll come back tomorrow night,' said Thomas.

He won the third night with eighteen out of twenty.

'A champion,' yelled the host. 'A true champion. Thomas Gulliver, you have won . . .'

Thomas didn't even listen.

He could see Mum and Dad on their feet. Mum seemed to want him to take this prize, whatever it was.

Sorry Mum, thought Thomas. You'd understand if you knew.

He waited for the compere to stop talking, then said he'd come back the next night.

At lunch in the hospitality room, the producer came over to where Thomas was sitting with Mum and Dad and the others.

Mum was in the middle of telling Thomas that she didn't really want a new kitchen, not really, and that granite workbenches were a bit flash for her.

Thomas was in the middle of having a nipple attack and a guilt attack.

'So, Tommo,' said the producer. 'Well done. You're a heck of a competitor.'

'Thanks,' said Thomas.

'He watches a lot of game shows,' said Alisha. 'We let him do it instead of going to school.'

'Very focussed,' said the producer to Thomas.

'I help him with that,' said Kevin.

'Bit of advice, Tommo,' said the producer. 'Try not to get so stressed when you get one wrong. You almost look like you're having a panic attack. Relax, buddy, everyone gets a few wrong.'

'Thanks,' said Thomas. 'I'll try to remember that.'

'So,' said the producer. 'Two more nights for the big prize. Do you think you can do it?'

'I think so,' said Thomas.

'I think so too,' said the producer, giving Thomas a pretend punch on the chin.

Thomas was glad it wasn't a pretend punch on the chest. His nipples had just gone feather duster.

The producer was lying.

Thomas won the fourth night with seventeen out of twenty.

As the compere led him over to the prize area, he whispered to Thomas.

'Take this one, son. You won't be winning anything else.'

The prize was a pair of jet skis and a pair of laser-guided harpoons.

When Thomas said no, the audience cheered. All except one voice up the back that groaned loudly.

Thomas wasn't sure, but he thought it might have been Kevin.

At the start of the final night, Thomas realised he had a problem.

Hot nipples.

All day they'd been getting hotter and hotter under the studio lights. Plus, each time a contestant buzzed *true* or *liar*, the wall of lights around the set flashed to show if the contestant was right or wrong.

Thomas felt like an all-beef patty being slowly grilled.

Sweat was trickling down his back. The microphone cable under his shirt was making him itch all over. The TV make-up powder on his face felt like baked mud. His chest was getting so overheated he could hardly tell when it was itching or not.

Plus he had nipple fatigue.

Each time a lie was told to a contestant, Thomas's nipples went into itch mode. They'd been double feather duster so many times over the last few hours, they were tingling almost full-time.

Concentrate, Thomas begged them. Don't let me down now.

The first round began.

The first contestant's Liar Liar was an Aussie Rules footballer wearing a cricket outfit.

Liar, liar, true, liar, true, buzzed the first contestant, and the wall of lights behind Thomas flashed as hot as ever. Thomas wondered if the cameras would spot him if he stuck his head down the front of his shirt and blew hard.

Probably.

The first contestant sat back in her seat. Thomas glanced at the scoreboard. Fifteen out of twenty.

I can beat that, he thought. As long as my nipples don't explode.

The compere introduced the second contestant. A bloke in a tracksuit who was a member of Australia's Olympic team.

The studio audience applauded as contestant two's Liar Liar appeared. She was a lady with big bosoms wearing only a very small bikini.

Lucky thing, thought Thomas. At least she's dressed for the climate in here.

The compere asked contestant number two if he'd ever met his Liar Liar before. It was the same question every contestant was asked.

'No,' said the Olympic athlete.

Thomas nearly fell off his stool.

His nipples were on red alert.

Contestant number two was lying.

This isn't fair, thought Thomas indignantly. If contestant number two has met his Liar Liar before, because she's a member of the Australian Olympic swimming team or something, he probably already knows what she's going to say and whether it's true or not.

That's cheating.

Thomas felt a powerful urge to dob.

A very powerful urge.

But he didn't. The producers had asked all the contestants to remember that they were on a family TV show, and not to do anything that would upset family viewers. Thomas was pretty sure that included dobbing.

Plus, Thomas reminded himself, there's the little matter that, technically, I'm cheating too.

He kept quiet. He hoped that the Olympic athlete had a bad memory and would only score sixteen or seventeen.

Liar, liar, liar, liar, true, true, liar, liar, true, liar, true, liar, true, liar, liar, liar, liar, liar, true, liar.

The Olympic athlete scored nineteen.

Thomas felt panic prickling his skin along with the sweat and make-up powder.

Nineteen was a lot.

To beat nineteen, he'd have to get a perfect score.

'Unbelievable,' whispered the compere.

He was in shock.

So, by the look of him, was the Olympic athlete.

'Never before,' said the compere, finding his

voice again, 'in the history of this show . . .'

The studio audience was cheering and hollering.

Thomas felt embarrassed. He hadn't wanted to get a perfect score, but he hadn't been given any choice.

Now he just wanted to choose his prize and go home.

After what seemed like an eternity of applause, with the compere talking so excitedly that Thomas was sprayed with saliva, they got to the prizes.

The grand prizes.

A beautiful brand-new shiny car that Thomas was surprised to see was here in the studio. It did look very nice. Thomas was pretty sure it wouldn't ever cough or lurch.

The other grand prize was on the TV monitors hanging from the studio ceiling. Exotic travel destinations. An all-expenses-paid trip for four to anywhere in the world.

'Which will it be?' asked the compere.

Thomas tried not to see Mum and Dad, but there they were, in the corner of his eye. Mum was mouthing 'car'. Dad was frantically moving his hands as if he was clutching a steering wheel.

Thomas looked away.

The compere was beaming at him, waiting.

'The trip, please,' said Thomas.

15

'Do planes crash much?' asked Kevin.

Thomas opened his eyes wearily. A flight attendant was leaning across his and Holly's seats, handing Kevin yet another can of lemonade.

'No,' said the flight attendant. 'Not much.'

As the flight attendant made her way back along the aisle, Thomas saw that Kevin was looking at him, waiting.

He knew what Kevin was waiting for.

'True,' said Thomas. 'She's telling the truth.'

Kevin looked relieved.

Holly sighed.

'This is getting ridiculous,' she said to Kevin. 'Give Thomas a break.'

Thomas could see what Holly was thinking. That there might be worse things than plane crashes and serious nipple conditions. Like having to sit next to Kevin for another nineteen hours.

Kevin was looking indignant.

'What do you mean, ridiculous?' he said.

'You know what I mean,' said Holly. 'We've only been flying for two hours. So far you've asked about the fuel consumption of the plane, how much pilots earn, whether the in-flight movies have the rude bits edited out, and what happens to the poo in the toilets while we're in mid-air.'

Kevin looked hurt.

'I was doing it for all of us,' he said. 'So we'd know the truth.'

'Thomas's nipples,' said Holly, 'are not toys. They're a rare and historic medical condition and we're travelling to Paris to find a cure, not to discover how the plumbing works on the plane.'

'It's alright for you,' said Kevin. 'You don't live under a flight path.'

Thomas sighed.

Even though it was still daytime, he was feeling strangely weary. And a bit ill. Could jetlag hit this quickly?

'Are you OK?' Holly asked him. 'You look sort of pale.'

'Just a bit tired,' said Thomas.

'You've been looking tired for two weeks now,' said Holly, concerned. 'Ever since the TV show. I reckon it took heaps out of you, winning all those nights in the one day.'

Thomas nodded. She could be right.

'Which is why, Kevin,' said Holly, 'you have to give Thomas a break.'

'You're not the boss of me,' said Kevin indignantly. 'You wouldn't even be on this trip if Thomas's sister wasn't staying behind to keep an eye on her boyfriend and if the TV show hadn't agreed to swap two business class tickets for three economy ones and if Miss Pearson hadn't told our parents that travel is an important part of education and if –'

'Neither of us would,' said Holly, glaring at Kevin. 'What's your point?'

Thomas closed his eyes.

'If you two don't stop arguing,' he said wearily, 'I'm going up the front to sit with Mum and Dad.'

'Sorry,' said Kevin.

'Sorry,' said Holly.

There was a short silence.

'The TV show was my idea,' murmured Kevin.

Thomas reminded himself that Kevin had family problems and needed special patience and understanding as well as non-stop lemonade.

Even so, nineteen more hours was feeling like a very long time.

Although he was very weary, Thomas couldn't sleep. He kept thinking about the things he'd miss if he was dead.

Mum and Dad and Alisha.

Holly and Kevin.

His room at home.

His invitation to Miss Pearson and Mr Demos's wedding.

The more things he thought of, the sadder he felt. So he made himself think about other things.

Why, he wondered, are planes so noisy?

They'd been flying for a few hours now and Thomas still hadn't got used to the faint non-stop roar that seemed to fill his head. He knew it was mostly the engines, but if he closed his eyes and listened carefully he thought he could also hear the distant sound of millions of people on the planet far below, all telling lies.

'How's it going, you three?'

Thomas opened his eyes.

It was Dad, crouching next to his seat.

'We're good, thanks,' said Thomas. 'What's it like in business class?'

'Do you get whole lobsters for every meal?' said Kevin, taking off his earphones. 'And champagne to wash in?'

Dad frowned.

'It's pretty nice,' he said. 'The seats are very comfy. There wouldn't be many new cars with seats that comfortable. But I'm more of a sandwich kind of bloke.'

'Seen any good movies?' asked Holly.

Dad shook his head.

'To tell the truth,' he said, 'I've been taking it a bit quietly. Having a bit of a think. Mum's watching *Toy Story 3*.'

Thomas saw a flicker of something in Dad's eyes. Unhappiness.

Worry.

Both those things and more.

'That car that was the prize on the TV show,' blurted Kevin. 'It's rubbish. My dad says they're really hard to park.'

Thomas and his nipples knew what Kevin was trying to do, and Thomas was grateful. He also wondered if you could strap a seatbelt across a person's mouth.

'Don't get me wrong,' said Dad. 'I'm having a great time. I'm a very lucky bloke to have a genius son.'

He ruffled Thomas's hair.

Thomas didn't know what to say, so he concentrated on not scratching his nipples. They'd gone mozzie bite the moment Dad said he was having a great time.

'Anyway,' said Dad, 'just wanted to check you're all OK. Be good.'

He headed back up the aisle towards the front of the plane.

Poor Dad, thought Thomas. He's got so much on his mind. No job. No new car. I hope this trip helps him feel better.

Holly put her hand on Thomas's arm.

'Unemployed people often feel depressed,' she said. 'My mum did an article on it. Foreign travel can help.'

Thomas gave her a grateful look.

'Your dad would probably enjoy the trip more,'

said Kevin, 'if he knew how it's gunna save your life.'

Thomas gave Kevin a pained look.

'Kevin,' said Holly. 'Unemployed people have got enough to worry about without knowing their kids are sick. Why don't you ask a flight attendant for some more lemonade?'

Everyone on the plane was asleep except Thomas.

And, he hoped, the pilots.

There were two reasons Thomas couldn't sleep.

Leg cramp, and worry.

The cramp felt a bit better when he wiggled his bottom and rubbed his knees, but the worry just kept getting worse.

What if he couldn't find Vera Poulet?

Or what if he found her but she didn't know why she was the only doubter who hadn't died young?

Or what if she did know but her survival technique was something impossible for Thomas to do, like waggling his ears or eating yoghurt?

Thomas felt Holly digging him gently with her elbow. He opened his eyes and saw she wasn't asleep either. She had her tray-table down and her laptop open. The screen was glowing in the gloom of the cabin.

'Sorry to disturb you,' whispered Holly. 'But we'll be in Paris in five hours and we need to work out what we're going to do.'

'Good thinking,' said Thomas.

'We land in Paris at six a.m.,' said Holly. 'Your mum and dad will probably be asleep with jetlag in the hotel by lunchtime. As soon as they are, we should go looking for Vera Poulet.'

'Good idea,' said Thomas. 'It might take us several hours if we have to eat yoghurt.'

'Eh?' said Holly. 'What's yoghurt got to do with it?'

'Sorry,' said Thomas. 'I mean if we get lost.'

What was happening to him? His brain felt like airline mashed potato. This was definitely jetlag.

'We won't get lost,' said Holly.

She clicked and a street map appeared on the screen.

'I downloaded this before we left,' she said. 'Look, there's the Denfert-Rochereau area where Vera Poulet works.'

Thomas saw where she was pointing. He could see the Avenue Denfert-Rochereau and the Place Denfert-Rochereau, but the map didn't seem to show pet-grooming parlours.

'What if we can't find exactly where she works?' asked Thomas.

'These'll help,' said Holly.

Thomas watched as she clicked through several photos of French pet-grooming parlours.

'Is one of those Vera Poulet's?' he asked, impressed.

'Fraid not,' said Holly. 'They're just examples of pet parlours in Paris so we know what we're looking for. But when we've found Vera Poulet's, in case she doesn't speak English, I've got this.'

Holly clicked again and the translation software window appeared on the screen.

Thomas grinned at her.

Incredible, he thought. And she hasn't even studied journalism at university or after-school care.

He was about to thank her when suddenly she clicked the screen blank.

Thomas realised Mum was crouching down next to them.

'Hi, kids,' said Mum. 'I can't sleep so I thought I'd come and see how you're going.'

'We're good, thanks,' said Thomas.

He knew why poor Mum couldn't sleep. Worry about the beauty salon. Worry about their old car. Worry about Alisha.

'You don't have to worry about Alisha,' said Thomas. 'She'll be fine.'

Mum frowned.

'I hope so,' she said. 'It's not like Alisha to put school work before fun. And I'm a bit nervous about how she'll go staying with Tanya's parents. They're very nice but they're vegetarian.'

Thomas wished he could explain to Mum that Alisha would definitely be OK. He'd asked Alisha if she was planning to wag school or have a baby with Garth or steal Tanya's dad's car or break into home and have a massive party with vomiting, and she'd said no. Thomas's nipples had stayed normal even when she'd given them several annoyed tweaks.

There was a flurry of kicking and stretching under the airline blanket next to Thomas.

Kevin emerged, blinking.

'Are you worried about that legal document you and Mr Gulliver had to sign?' he said to Mum. 'The one that gets you into big trouble if Thomas cheated on the TV show? You don't have to worry, my Dad knows some top lawyers.'

Thomas winced.

Seatbelt across his mouth, definitely.

But it was OK. Mum was smiling at Kevin.

'No, love,' she said. 'I'm not worried about that. I pluck a solicitor's eyebrows, so I know about legal stuff. And anyway, how could Thomas have cheated?'

Thomas prayed Kevin wouldn't say anything else.

'No,' Mum continued, giving Thomas's arm a loving squeeze. 'What I've been thinking about in my lovely comfy business-class seat is how I haven't thanked you properly, Thomas, for winning us this wonderful trip.'

She kissed him on the cheek.

Thomas felt weak with relief.

'You're welcome,' he said.

'Tell me one thing,' said Mum. 'Dad and I think we've worked it out, but we want to be sure. Why did you choose the trip instead of the car?'

Thomas felt the panic return.

He'd rehearsed this moment, and now it had finally come he couldn't remember which answer he'd decided on. Was it the one about wanting to give Mum and Dad the honeymoon they'd never had, or the one about how Mum could pick up French beauty techniques in Paris for the salon?

'Um . . .' he said.

He saw that Holly didn't know what to say either.

Then Kevin spoke up.

'Thomas is doing it for me, Mrs Gulliver,' he said. 'It's to help me get over my nan's death.'

Thomas stared at Kevin.

'She died after a trip to France,' said Kevin. 'From food poisoning. Which she got in Paris.'

There was a long silence. Thomas watched Mum think about this. She was still crouched down next to him and he desperately hoped she couldn't feel the massive itchy vibrations coming off his nipples.

'I'm sorry to hear that, Kevin,' said Mum. 'When did your nan die?'

Kevin hesitated.

'Um . . . last year,' he said. 'Or the year before.'

Mum didn't say anything. Thomas held his breath. After a few moments he realised Mum wasn't speaking because she was feeling emotional.

She reached over and patted Kevin on the arm. Then she put her arms round Thomas and squeezed him tight.

'You're a very kind and thoughtful boy,' she

murmured into Thomas's ear. 'Letting Kevin think you're doing this for him. And you're a wonderful son for letting me and Dad finally have a honeymoon.'

'Thanks,' said Thomas.

He didn't know what else to say.

Mum stood up and gave them all a warm smile.

'Even though it's not the best time for me to be going overseas,' she said, 'I think we're all going to have a very happy week. And I'm going to share a secret with you. One of the things me and Dad have always wanted to do is have a picnic under the Eiffel Tower in Paris.'

Thomas couldn't believe what he was hearing.

It was the perfect way to take Mum and Dad's minds off their problems.

He waited while Mum went back to her seat, then gave Kevin a grateful grin and saw that Holly was doing the same.

Kevin's right, thought Thomas. I worry too much. With friends like I've got, everything's going to be fine.

As long as I can stay alive.

16

The Paris metro was amazing.

A gleaming underground train with rubber wheels hissed out of a tunnel and sped towards the platform in gusts of warm air that smelled of garlic.

Thomas knew if he wasn't feeling so strange he'd be enjoying it as much as the other two.

'Brilliant,' said Kevin as they got into a crowded carriage where you didn't have to sit down, you could stand up and hang off plastic handles if you wanted.

'It's very clean,' said Holly as the train accelerated into the tunnel without a single cough or lurch.

'Wow,' said Kevin as the tunnel walls started to flash by at speeds unheard of in Australian tunnels.

'What a well laid out urban transport system,' said Holly as she studied the plan of the Paris metro above the carriage door. But between gazes she threw anxious glances at Thomas.

Thomas didn't want to spoil the experience for Holly, so he tried not to look too weary.

'Six more stops to Denfert-Rochereau,' he said, studying the plan with her.

'It's dead quiet,' said Kevin. 'For a train.'

Thomas didn't say anything.

Kevin was probably right, but Thomas couldn't tell because his head was still full of the fuzzy roaring sound from the plane.

In the taxi from the airport he'd told himself it was just the echo of the jet engines in his brain.

'It'll fade,' Holly had told him at the hotel when he'd mentioned it to her.

But it hadn't faded.

It was getting stronger.

Thomas closed his eyes and let the rubber wheels of the train whisper to him through the weird worrying noise in his head.

'Doubters, doubters, doubters,' they said. 'Die, die, die. Young, young, young.'

Thomas didn't blame the wheels. In fact he felt grateful to them.

They were speeding him closer to Vera Poulet.

The woman in the Denfert-Rochereau pet-grooming parlour stared at Thomas and Holly and Kevin as if they were scruffy pets in urgent need of grooming.

Thomas understood why.

It was a very expensive pet-grooming parlour, full of expensive furniture and expensive sinks and expensive smells. The French people going past outside on the wide elegant tree-lined street were wearing expensive French clothes and driving expensive French cars. The expensive pets being groomed inside the parlour looked like they'd already been groomed, at great expense, about ten minutes ago.

Amazing, thought Thomas. This place is twice as flash as Mum's salon, and she does people.

Thomas caught sight of himself and Holly and Kevin in a big mirror. They didn't look French, or expensive. They looked like they'd recently got off a plane after a twenty-two hour trip without a comb or an iron between them.

Vera Poulet will understand, thought Thomas. Once she realises who we are.

'Excuse me,' he said to the woman. 'Are you Vera Poulet?'

She didn't look much like the photo of Vera Poulet on Holly's computer, but Mum had explained to Thomas years ago that people could look quite different with their hair done or a good moisturiser.

The woman was frowning.

'*Nous chercher Vera Poulet,*' said Holly, reading from her laptop.

'*Non,*' said the woman crossly. '*Pas ici.*'

Thomas knew she was telling the truth. His nipples weren't even tingling. Unlike the nipples of the poodle being shampooed nearby, which were quivering with indignation at being interrupted by scruffs.

'*Salon de chouchou de Denfert-Rochereau?*' asked Holly, reading from her screen again.

'*Quoi?*' said the woman, sounding even crosser. '*Non.*'

Still no nipple itch.

Thomas turned away, disappointed. This woman wasn't Vera Poulet and this place wasn't the Denfert-Rochereau pet-grooming parlour.

'We're here about his nipples,' said Kevin loudly to the woman. 'Nipples.'

'*Allez-vous en!*' shouted the woman. '*Allez immediatement. J'appelle les autorités.*'

'Let's get out of here,' said Kevin. 'She's gunna call the cops.'

'Do you speak French?' Thomas asked him as they ran outside.

'No,' said Kevin. 'But when people threaten to call the police, my nipples itch.'

An hour later, in a quiet back street somewhere in the Denfert-Rochereau area, Thomas pressed his aching head against the wall of a shuttered apartment building and begged Paris to be honest with him.

'Please,' he whispered.

He didn't go into detail. There wasn't time to explain everything to Paris. How Mum and Dad would panic if they woke up from their afternoon nap in the hotel and found he and Holly and Kevin had snuck off. How Vera Poulet had information about doubters that Thomas desperately needed if he was going to stay alive much longer.

'We need to find the Denfert-Rochereau pet-grooming parlour,' he whispered. 'To cure my nipples.'

Thomas felt a bit dopey talking to a city, but he was desperate.

When you got away from the main boulevards, the street layout in Paris was very confusing. Narrow alleyways that just stopped at dead ends. Cobbled car parks that weren't on the map. Signposts that pointed at brick walls or other signposts.

Kevin was squatting on the ground again, moaning about sore feet and hunger pains.

Holly was frowning at the map on her laptop screen again, like she had in the last forty-seven streets they'd been in.

'We're lost,' she groaned.

'Great,' said Kevin. 'If I don't find some jelly snakes soon I'm gunna pass out.'

'I'm sorry,' said Holly to Thomas. 'On the plane I said this wouldn't happen.'

'It's not your fault,' said Thomas.

Then suddenly he had an idea. It was obvious. Why hadn't he thought of it before?

'Maybe we're looking for the wrong place,' he said.

'What do you mean?' said Holly.

'Vera Poulet works at the Denfert-Rochereau Catacombs, right?'

'Right,' said Holly.

'If she's still there,' said Kevin gloomily.

'Listen,' said Thomas. 'Maybe it's not a pet-grooming parlour. Maybe the computer translated it wrong. Maybe a catacombs isn't a place where cats get combed.'

'Of course it is,' said Kevin. 'Get real.'

'No,' said Holly, staring at Thomas. 'You could be right.'

'Let's ask someone,' said Thomas.

'Oh no,' wailed Kevin. 'We're not going all the way back to that main street where the crowds are. The one without the jelly snakes.'

'No need,' said Thomas. 'We'll ask someone in this street.'

The street was deserted.

Thomas went over to the entrance of the nearest apartment building and pressed all the brass doorbell buttons several times each.

He was still doing it when one of the upper window shutters banged open and a woman started shouting angrily at him in French.

'Sorry to bother you,' Thomas called up to her when she paused for breath. 'Do you speak English?'

The woman threw an empty milk carton which hit Thomas on the head. He assumed that meant she didn't.

'Catacombs,' he shouted to the woman.

An onion whistled past his head.

'Catacombs,' he pleaded. 'Please.'

'*S'il vous plaît*,' shouted Holly, reading from her laptop screen.

Thomas wondered if they could get the computer to speak to the woman.

Forget it.

'Catacombs,' he repeated more loudly, in case the woman had a hearing problem.

She obviously didn't. She finished what she was doing, which was throwing a turnip at Thomas, then paused and stared hard at the three of them.

After a moment she pointed up the street, saying something in French that sounded less angry.

Thomas waited for his nipples to detect she was lying.

They didn't.

She wasn't.

'Thank you,' he called to the woman.

'*Merci*,' said Holly.

They headed up the street in the direction the woman had pointed. Thomas swapped grins with Holly and Kevin.

It was a start.

It was more than a start.

At the end of the street and round the corner, they saw a signpost.

Denfert-Rochereau Ossuary.

It was pointing to a shiny black metal door in an old stone building. On the door was another sign.

Entrée Des Catacombes.

17

Thomas pulled open the black metal door of the Denfert-Rochereau Catacombs, went inside and found himself standing in front of a small ticket booth.

Sitting inside it was an elderly woman.

She didn't look much like the photo of Vera Poulet on Holly's computer, but Mum had explained to Thomas years ago that a bad hairdo could change your appearance even more than dry skin.

'Vera Poulet?' asked Thomas.

His chest was tingling. Not with nipple itch, with excitement.

'*En bas*,' said the woman, pointing downwards.

Thomas was confused.

Then he panicked.

Did she mean Vera Poulet was dead and buried? Was he too late to discover how to survive as a doubter? Because if he was, he'd probably be dead and buried himself fairly soon.

As Thomas struggled to stay calm, he felt Holly tapping him on the shoulder. She was pointing to some stone steps leading down into a stairwell.

'I think she means Vera Poulet is down there,' said Holly.

Thomas felt dizzy with relief. He hurried over to the steps. There was a turnstile blocking his way.

'*N'oubliez pas les billets*,' called the woman in the ticket booth. '*Excusez-moi*.'

'She doesn't want us to run down the steps,' said Kevin. 'And she doesn't want any excuses.'

'Possibly,' said Holly. 'But what she's saying is we have to buy tickets.'

Thomas could feel the air getting colder and damper as the three of them plodded down the spiral stone steps. It felt like they were descending into the chill depths of the earth.

'What is this place?' whispered Holly.

'Maybe it's where people come to check out the Paris sewers,' said Kevin. 'You know, if you drop something down the toilet and want to get it back.'

Thomas wished he'd looked at the information on the wall next to the ticket booth. Some of it might have been in English. But OK, there were times when you didn't stop to read instructions. Getting a new video game, for example, or meeting the person who could save your life.

At last they came to the bottom of the steps.

Ahead of them was a long gloomy tunnel.

Thomas didn't hesitate. He headed off into the gloom with Holly and Kevin close behind him.

Then he had a thought and stopped and turned to them.

'I'm really grateful you're both here,' he said. 'But if it gets too scary and you want to go back up, I'll understand.'

In the dim light he could see Holly's eyes, big and truthful.

'Don't be a dope,' she said quietly.

'Yeah,' said Kevin. 'Don't be.'

'Thanks,' said Thomas.

He really meant it. He was feeling so jetlagged now, so weary and noisy in the head, that he wasn't sure how much longer he could keep going on his own.

They trudged into the tunnel.

A small voice whispered in the gloom.

It was Kevin's.

'Why might it get too scary?'

Thomas decided the tunnel wasn't a sewer, it was too dry for that.

Which was a relief.

It meant the fuzzy roaring in his head was still just the fuzzy roaring in his head, and not the distant sound of millions of litres of sewage hurtling along the tunnel towards them.

'Look at the walls,' said Holly.

Every few metres there was a dull light in a metal bracket on the tunnel wall, and in each patch of light Thomas could see how the tunnel had been chipped out of the rock by hand.

'It must have taken ages,' said Holly.

'Almost as long as it's taking us to get to wherever we're going,' said Kevin.

Thomas plodded on and tried not to think about Mum and Dad getting worried.

'I think I know what this place is,' said Holly suddenly. 'My parents told me how wine and champagne in France is often stored underground in old tunnels that go for kilometres.'

'Great,' said Kevin. 'Did they say how many kilometres?'

Thomas had a thought.

Maybe that's how Vera Poulet had survived being a doubter and avoided dying young. By drinking lots of champagne.

He shook his head.

Silly idea.

Why couldn't he think properly any more?

Was it jetlag or something worse?

Suddenly Thomas heard voices. Low murmuring voices. Coming from around a corner up ahead where the tunnel joined a bigger tunnel.

He took a deep breath and stepped into the bigger tunnel.

And gasped.

So did Holly.

Kevin gave a squeak.

Neatly stacked along the walls of this tunnel, from floor to roof, were thousands and thousands of bones.

Millions of them. And not just kid millions, thought Thomas, stunned. Real millions. The tunnel was long and high and for as far as Thomas could see ahead, the walls were all bones.

Thin bones.

Thick bones.

Towering stacks of them.

Row upon row of skulls.

'Human skulls,' whispered Holly, her voice wobbly.

Thomas could see human arm bones too. And human leg bones. And human rib bones.

'Jeez,' whispered Kevin. 'My dad always reckons drinking too much wine is bad for your health. Wait till I tell him about this place.'

'This isn't a wine cellar,' said Holly. 'I don't know what it is.'

'I'll tell you,' said a deep voice with a French accent.

Thomas spun round, startled.

Sitting on a wooden chair under one of the lights was an elderly man in a uniform. He had black skin and grey whiskers.

'These are the bones,' said the man, stretching out his arms, 'of seven million people. They all lived and died in Paris hundreds of years ago. They were buried in old cemeteries all over the city. When the cemetery lands were needed for new houses, their bones were dug up and brought down here to these old quarry tunnels.'

Thomas realised who the man must be.

An attendant, like in a museum, to make sure people didn't take any of the bones home for their dogs.

'Any questions?' said the attendant.

Thomas only had one.

'Vera Poulet?' he asked.

The attendant looked surprised. Then he pointed along the tunnel of bones.

The woman attendant was sitting on a chair as well. She was wearing a uniform like the man attendant and she was about as old as he was, and she had roughly as many wrinkles as he did.

Everything else about her, Thomas saw as he approached, was different.

She was taller than the man, even when she was sitting down. Her face was thin and serious, not smiley like his. Her hair was white and pinned up into a tight bun. Her arms were folded and she didn't even glance at Thomas and Holly and Kevin, not even when they got close to her.

Unlike the man, she looked very similar to the photo of Vera Poulet on Holly's computer.

'Excuse me,' Thomas said to her, trembling with excitement.

'*Excusement-moi*,' said Holly, reading from the laptop.

The woman continued to stare at the bones in front of her, which were glowing spookily in the light from the laptop screen.

'Are you Vera Poulet?' said Thomas softly.

'*Être-vous Vera Poulet?*' read Holly.

The woman still ignored them.

'If you are,' said Kevin, 'give us a sign. Blink three times.'

'Hang on,' said Holly, tapping her laptop keys. 'I can't keep up. What came after blink?'

Thomas saw it didn't matter. The woman was still ignoring them.

He stood right in front of her.

'Go away,' she said, closing her eyes.

Thomas wondered for a second if she was ill. He decided she wasn't. Just very unfriendly.

'Please,' said Thomas. 'It's really important. I need to find out about the doubters.'

Now she looked at him. Sharply and suspiciously.

'*Je voudrais*,' read Holly, '*les informations . . .*'

'I speak English,' said the woman, looking away again.

'We've come from Australia,' said Thomas. 'To see you.'

The woman blew out an exasperated breath of air. She kept her arms folded.

'So,' she said. 'An old article in a dead magazine finds its way to Australia. And now you are wanting

138

to know about *les* doubters.'

'Yes,' whispered Thomas.

He was feeling weak and dizzy, and he didn't know if it was because he was jetlagged or sick or just because he'd finally found Vera Poulet.

'Doubters are children,' said Vera Poulet. She spoke in the dull voice of someone who'd said it all heaps of times before. 'Children whose bodies speak to them about lies. Children with itchy wrists. Trembling legs. Painful hearts. Hot noses. Children whose bodies are . . . how do you say?'

'Lie-detectors,' said Thomas.

'Yes,' said Vera Poulet, looking at him in surprise. 'That's what they are exactly.'

'We need to know,' said Holly. 'Why do doubters die young?'

Vera Poulet stared at the walls of bones all around them.

For a crazy, dizzy moment Thomas thought she was going to say that these millions of bones were all the remains of doubters.

No, that was silly.

'The more lies the young bodies of doubters absorb,' said Vera Poulet, 'the more their immune systems are damaged. The more easily they become sick. In centuries past there were no antibiotics. Sick children always died.'

Thomas crouched down, suddenly giddy. The noise in his head was getting louder. And now he knew it wasn't jetlag.

'You were a doubter,' said Holly urgently to Vera Poulet. 'You didn't die. How come?'

Thomas looked up at Vera Poulet and saw a flicker of something in her eyes.

Confusion.

Fear.

Both those things and more.

'If the lies stop,' she said, 'the lies of families and communities, sometimes the health of the doubters can recover.'

'And that's how you survived?' said Thomas.

Vera Poulet nodded.

'My powers faded when I was twelve,' she said. 'But I am always at risk. The powers, and the sickness, they could return.'

'But they haven't,' said Holly. 'Have they?'

Thomas was shocked by the anger that suddenly flashed across Vera Poulet's face.

'The sickness could come back at any time,' she snapped.

Then, as her voice echoed down the tunnel of bones, she hunched her shoulders again and looked away.

'Enough,' she said. 'You don't need to know more.'

'Yes, we do,' said Kevin. 'We need to know everything. And you might as well tell us the truth, cause we've got nipples here that'll dob you.'

'He means nipples that'll tell us if you're lying,' said Holly.

Vera Poulet's eyes widened.

She stared at all three of them.

For the first time, Thomas saw, she unfolded her arms.

'Which one of you . . .?' she whispered.

'Me,' said Thomas.

18

Vera Poulet was a fast walker.

Thomas struggled to keep up as they turned a corner into yet another street. He could see Holly and Kevin were panting too.

'Are you OK?' said Holly.

Thomas didn't feel good, but he felt better than before.

His head was still noisy, but he wasn't as dizzy. Hopeful thoughts were keeping him going, along with the jelly snakes Kevin had just ducked into a shop and bought.

'I'm fine, thanks,' Thomas said to Holly.

He ignored the nipple itch he got when he said that. The important thing was getting to Vera Poulet's place.

'I wonder why she wants us to go to her home?' said Holly.

'Der,' said Kevin. 'To help Thomas, of course. She's probably got medicine there. Or bulk spinach juice for a special doubters' diet.'

'Der yourself,' said Holly. 'She already explained that the cure hasn't got anything to do with medicine or diets. What cures a doubter is when they don't have to listen to any more lies. Perhaps you should remember that, Kevin Abbot.'

Kevin stared at Holly, outraged, his mouth open.

Thomas looked away so he wouldn't have to see the half-chewed jelly snakes.

'I don't tell lies to Thomas,' said Kevin. 'Only to other people.'

Thomas sighed wearily.

'Please,' he said. 'Stop arguing. Vera Poulet reckons she's got something at her place that'll help me and that's all I care about. It probably isn't far.'

'Four kilometres,' said Vera Poulet.

Thomas was shocked. Vera Poulet was several steps ahead of them. He hadn't realised her hearing was that good.

'Why don't we catch the metro?' said Kevin.

'No metro,' said Vera Poulet, striding on. 'Too risky. Too full of people telling lies. My sickness could come back.'

Suddenly she veered off the footpath and hurried across the street.

Thomas realised why.

She wanted to get away from the electrical shop on this side. It had a TV out the front, showing a news report. The leader of China or India or somewhere was saying that the uranium they'd just bought would never be used for bombs or fighting or anything.

Thomas and the others crossed over too.

After a bit, as they approached a restaurant with tables out on the footpath, Vera Poulet strode back across the street.

'Bad restaurant,' she said to Thomas and the others as they followed.

'Why?' said Kevin. 'Don't they do chips?'

'They are famous for their Chilean sea bass,' said Vera Poulet with a snort of disgust. 'There is no such fish as Chilean sea bass. The real name of this fish is Patagonian tooth fish.'

Thomas felt dread sapping his energy.

Is this what his future would be like if he managed to stay alive? A whole lifetime of running and hiding from lies?

Vera Poulet's place was a dusty old apartment full of books and saggy furniture.

Thomas stood in the living room with Holly and Kevin, watching while Vera Poulet spoke in French to an elderly man slumped in an armchair.

The man stared grumpily at Thomas.

He said something in French, and Vera Poulet snorted at him like he was a Chilean sea bass.

Then she stepped over to Thomas.

'I should have explained to you,' she said. 'My husband was a vet. Now he is a liar.'

Thomas wasn't sure what to say.

He could see Holly and Kevin were surprised too.

If Monsieur Poulet was a vet, you'd expect him to be tall and kind and gentle and well groomed like the vets on telly. Not short and unshaven and cross in a droopy jumper that looked suspiciously to Thomas like it was made from animal hair.

'*Bonjour*,' Monsieur Poulet snapped at Thomas and the others. '*Ça va?*'

'English,' said Vera Poulet impatiently. 'Speak English to them.'

Monsieur Poulet gave a grumpy growl.

'I retire since twelveteen years,' he said crossly. 'Not since twelveteen years do I speak English. Or animal.'

'Well you can start again now,' said Vera Poulet to him, just as crossly.

Monsieur Poulet muttered something under his breath in French. Thomas was having trouble concentrating because of the noise in his head, but he was pretty sure it was a swear word.

'English,' said Vera Poulet.

'Bottom plops,' said Monsieur Poulet. He glared at his wife. 'It is the only English swearing word I know.'

'There's lots more,' said Kevin. 'I can write some down for you if you like.'

There was an awkward silence.

'Madame Poulet,' said Holly. 'You said you have something to help Thomas?'

'Yes,' said Vera Poulet, with another glare at her husband. 'I'll get it.'

As soon as she was out of the room, Monsieur Poulet stood up and came over to Thomas.

Suddenly his face seemed gentler.

'So, young man,' he said. 'You are a doubter.'

Thomas nodded.

'*Incroyable*,' said Monsieur Poulet. 'Thank God. At last.'

Monsieur Poulet was looking so emotional that Thomas felt he should say something himself.

'Mrs Poulet is very kind,' he said. 'She's helping me.'

Monsieur Poulet thought about this. He gave a snort very much like his wife's.

Only sadder.

'My wife, what she needs is someone helping her,' he said. 'She needs the understanding that she is OK. That the lies cannot hurt her now. That she does not have to hide away under the ground with the bones. That she is not the doubter any more.'

Thomas didn't know what to say.

His nipples stayed silent too.

Monsieur Poulet was telling the truth.

'I try to speak her myself,' continued Monsieur Poulet. 'I am medical expert. I have done the research. Only the children can be doubters. When the sickness fades, it never comes back. She is safe. But since fifty years she doesn't believe this.'

Thomas was shocked to see that Monsieur

Poulet was almost in tears.

Then Vera Poulet's voice rang out.

'He's lying, isn't he, Thomas?'

Thomas turned. Vera Poulet was standing in the doorway, holding a battered cardboard folder, looking at her husband. Her face was sadder than any face Thomas had ever seen.

With a jolt, Thomas realised why she'd brought him here. It wasn't just so she could help him. It was so he could also help her.

'My husband is lying, isn't he?' Vera Poulet repeated.

'No,' said Thomas. 'He's telling the truth.'

For a few seconds Vera Poulet's face relaxed. But only for a few seconds.

'Pah,' she snorted again. 'This is the problem. He thinks he is telling the truth, but he's not.'

'I am telling the truth,' said Monsieur Poulet to Thomas. 'But she's right, I do lie to her. She doesn't know, but each day I tell her a little lie. I read her from the newspaper and change one little fact each day. To prove that her sickness will never come back.'

He waved his arms in the air.

'No, *non, nada, niet*,' he said. 'How many languages does she want me to say it? Since fifty years she is only a doubter *dans la tête*.'

'In the head,' said Holly, reading from her laptop.

'Fifty years,' said Kevin. 'That is mega sad.'

Thomas looked at Vera Poulet. She was trembling, holding on to the door frame.

'Tell me,' she said to Thomas, her voice trembling too. 'Is he lying now?'

'No,' said Thomas.

Vera Poulet stared at her husband for a long time. Then she took a few uncertain steps across the room and sat down on the couch, head bowed.

Monsieur Poulet sat down next to her and put his arms around her. She took his hand and pressed it to her cheek.

Thomas saw the tears on both their faces.

Holly and Kevin were watching, close to tears themselves. Thomas knew how they felt. Even though his head was killing him.

'Come on,' he whispered to them. 'We should go.'

'What about the folder?' whispered Holly.

'Create a diversion,' whispered Kevin. 'I'll nick it.'

But he didn't have to.

Vera Poulet stood up and brought it over to Thomas.

'Thank you,' she said, looking at him with bright watery eyes. She pushed the folder into his hands. 'In here is research about the sickness. Everything we have. History, geography, medical, everything.'

She paused and put her hand on Thomas's forehead.

Her hand felt cool and Thomas realised how hot his head was.

'The cure is very simple,' said Vera Poulet. 'The people close to you who are telling the lies, they must stop.'

Thomas nodded.

'Thank you,' he said.

It's what he had feared she would say.

19

'How much longer do we have to keep these blindfolds on?' said Dad, fiddling with the airline sleeping-mask over his eyes.

'Be patient,' said Mum, adjusting her own sleeping-mask. 'It's a surprise.'

'We're nearly there,' said Thomas, trying to sound cheerful.

It wasn't easy. After a night of bad sleep and scary dreams he felt even more exhausted and weary than yesterday in the catacombs. Plus the noise in his head was louder than ever, even after two headache tablets.

'*Deux minutes,*' said the taxi driver.

'Two minutes,' said Holly, reading from her laptop screen.

Thomas hugged the picnic basket he'd borrowed from the hotel and peered through the taxi window at the sky. It was still grey, but at least the rain had stopped.

Come on sun, begged Thomas silently. Please. I need your help. Mum and Dad are going to have some nasty surprises in a minute, and a bit of sunshine might help them cope better.

Thomas glanced at the taxi meter. Eleven euros. He hoped the taxi driver was right about almost being there. Thomas only had fourteen euros of his holiday money left after buying the picnic food.

'I wonder where we're going,' said Mum.

'I'm wondering that too,' said Dad.

The taxi turned a corner and suddenly Thomas could see it above them, bigger than he'd ever imagined, the most famous tower in the world.

The Eiffel Tower.

It wasn't what Thomas had expected at all.

He'd imagined something like a castle tower, with flowers growing over it and perhaps a fountain on top. Something romantic. This one looked like it was built of metal girders.

'Wow,' gasped Kevin. 'It's huge. And it's built of metal girders.'

Thomas glared at him.

Holly slapped her hand over Kevin's mouth.

'It's a surprise,' she hissed at him.

Thomas wished they had a spare sleeping-mask to use as a gag.

'Sorry,' mumbled Kevin.

'*Voilà*,' said the taxi driver, pulling in to the kerb.

Holly wasn't able to translate because she still

had her computer hand over Kevin's mouth, but Thomas was pretty sure it was French for *Great spot for a surprise picnic. Your parents are going to love it. They probably won't even get upset when they find out why you've brought them here.*

'Thanks,' said Thomas as he paid the taxi driver. 'I hope you're right.'

'OK,' said Thomas. 'Three, two, one, blindfolds off.'

He held his breath and also the tablecloth, which was flapping a bit in the wind. Holly removed Mum's sleeping-mask, and after a bit of fiddling Kevin got Dad's off.

Thomas watched as Mum and Dad looked around, and then up.

Their mouths fell open.

They looked at Thomas, then at each other, then at the picnic food laid out on the tablecloth, then around again at the four massive pillars supporting the tower, then up again at the dizzying lattice of girders disappearing into the clouds.

'Surprise,' said Kevin, unnecessarily in Thomas's opinion.

Mum and Dad couldn't be more surprised. Their mouths were still wide open.

'Oh, love,' said Mum to Thomas. 'You remembered what I said on the plane. Thank you. You're amazing.'

'He certainly is,' grinned Dad. 'One in a million.'

Thomas felt a bit less tense. Except for his head, which was still full of fuzzy noise.

While Mum and Dad gave him a hug, Thomas had a thought. If today didn't work, if he still ended up dying young, at least Mum and Dad would have happy picnic memories to help them feel not quite so sad.

OK, the setting wasn't as beautiful as Thomas had wanted. The ground under the tower wasn't the grass with daisies and buttercups he'd hoped for, it was concrete with puddles. Also the wind was blowing great gobs of water off the upper part of the tower and they were plummeting onto the picnic food. And lots of the tourists queuing for the lifts were staring in a not very beautiful way.

But it wasn't all bad. Mum and Dad were sitting on a very nice wooden bench bolted into the concrete so they didn't get their bottoms wet. And the hotel shower-curtain tablecloth was completely waterproof. Plus, Holly and Kevin were making it windproof by sitting on the corners.

Right, thought Thomas.

Food first.

He'd discussed this with Holly and Kevin, and they'd agreed that people probably cope better with nasty surprises when they're enjoying the finest food a country or region can offer.

'Snail?' said Thomas, holding a paper plate out to Mum and Dad.

Mum and Dad stared at the pile of oily snails in

their garlic-flecked shells.

'It's OK,' said Kevin. 'They're cooked.'

'Kevin,' said Holly. 'Mr and Mrs Gulliver know they're cooked. As the man in the deli explained to us this morning, *escargots* are one of the greatest delicacies in France, but only an idiot would eat them raw.'

'Um,' said Dad. 'Yes. Fantastic. Thank you.'

'This is a lovely surprise,' said Mum. 'Thank you, all three of you. No wonder you were gone so long yesterday.'

Mum and Dad took a snail each.

Dad took a deep breath, put his snail to his lips, sucked hard and swallowed as fast as he could.

Mum sniffed hers, poked her tongue a little way inside the shell, pulled it out again and did lots of nodding and lip-smacking.

'Delicious,' said Dad.

'Yum,' said Mum.

Thomas's nipples went garlic prawn.

Or should that be garlic snail, he thought miserably.

Then he realised what the problem was. The snails probably weren't cooked enough. Mum and Dad liked their chops and fish fingers very well done.

'You'll like this tripe sausage,' said Thomas, holding out another plate. 'It's cooked a lot. They have to because of the germs.'

He could have kicked himself. Why had he said that?

Mum and Dad nibbled a slice each.

'Mmmm,' said Mum, struggling to sound happy.

'Mmmm,' said Dad, struggling even harder.

Thomas's nipples were going off like fire alarms.

'Try the cheese,' said Holly.

Thomas hastily unwrapped the small round cheese that the man in the deli had promised was another of the most popular delicacies in France. The smell was a bit of a worry, but Thomas had consulted his nipples in the shop and they'd said the deli man was telling the truth.

'It's goats' cheese,' said Holly.

'Yuk,' said Kevin.

Now the wrapper was off, Thomas saw why Kevin was looking disgusted and why Mum and Dad were too.

The small disc of cheese was covered with white and grey furry stuff.

Mould.

Thomas felt his own internal organs go sausage-shaped.

It wasn't working. The picnic wasn't working. And his head was almost exploding.

'This is a lovely thought, love,' Mum was saying as she peered nervously at the duck-fat sandwich-spread and the blood sausage and the pigs' feet in jelly. 'But I must still be a bit jetlagged because I don't actually feel very hungry.'

'Me neither,' said Dad. 'I had steak and eggs for breakfast.'

'No, you didn't,' said Kevin. 'You had muesli with the rest of us.'

'I had it in my room,' said Dad. 'Before I came down to breakfast. That's why you didn't see me eating it.'

A big drop of wind-blown water smacked onto Thomas's head and dribbled down the front of his shirt onto his nipples. It wasn't enough to stop them going triple feather duster, but it helped remind Thomas what he had to do.

He took a deep breath.

His head was roaring inside and he was feeling weaker and dizzier by the second.

He felt Holly's hand on his, squeezing, giving him strength.

'Do you know what I'd really like to do?' said Mum suddenly. 'We've been in Paris nearly a whole day and we haven't given a thought to Kevin's nan. We should do something in her memory. Why don't we buy some flowers and have a little memorial ceremony? We could do it down by the river.'

'Good idea,' said Dad.

Mum and Dad stood up.

Thomas stared at them in panic.

He had to make them stay, to hear what he had to tell them, but his head was throbbing so much he wasn't sure if he could even stand up.

'What do you think, Kevin?' said Mum.

Thomas stared at Kevin, silently pleading with him to say he hated the idea. He could see Holly was doing the same.

Kevin looked at Thomas for a moment, then stood up.

'That's a really nice idea,' he said to Mum and Dad. 'But my nan's not dead. She lives in Grafton.'

Thomas didn't need his nipples to know that Kevin was telling the truth.

Mum and Dad stared at Kevin, stunned.

'You lied?' said Dad.

Kevin nodded.

'But why . . .?' said Mum.

'He did it for me,' said Thomas.

Mum and Dad were looking at him now.

Thomas struggled to stay sitting upright.

'I was the one who needed to come to Paris,' said Thomas. 'Because the lies in our family are making me ill.'

'Ill?' said Mum, alarmed.

'Lies?' said Dad, looking alarmed too and also nervous. 'What lies?'

Thomas thought about Holly and Kevin and how much they'd helped him since he'd told them about his nipples. It could be the same for Mum and Dad. They could help each other with their secrets.

'Your job,' said Thomas to Dad.

Dad opened his mouth.

'The job you've been pretending you've still got,' said Thomas, before Dad could tell another lie.

Mum looked at Dad, horrified.

'You've lost your job?' she said.

'Oh, Jeez,' said Dad.

'Why didn't you tell me?' said Mum.

Dad didn't say anything, but Thomas could see the energy seeping out of Dad's face until it looked like a blood sausage without the blood.

'And Mum,' said Thomas. 'Why didn't you tell Dad the beauty salon's going broke?'

Dad's eyes went wide.

'Going broke?' he said. 'We put our life savings into that business.'

Mum turned away. Her shoulders slowly sagged until she looked like a snail without its shell.

'The salon's not going broke,' she said quietly. 'It's . . . it's already gone broke. I closed it down last week.'

Thomas saw the misery on Mum's face and the fear and panic on Dad's.

Oh no, he thought. What have I done?

He knew the answer. There was no point lying to himself. He hadn't made things better, he'd made them worse.

The noise in his head was like a plane crashing. Above him the huge tower seemed to be wobbling and twisting like it was made of jelly snakes.

He saw Mum and Dad and Holly and Kevin all looking at him. Their faces were wobbling and twisting as well, with alarm.

Thomas struggled to speak. He had to explain to

Mum and Dad. He had to tell them what he should have told them ages ago.

'I've been lying too,' he tried to say.

He tried to get Vera Poulet's cardboard folder from the picnic basket, but he couldn't reach it.

The sky was going dark.

People were saying his name but he couldn't see them any more.

The tower came crashing down onto him and he felt himself dying young.

20

Thomas opened his eyes.

For a moment he couldn't remember where he was.

Then he did.

'*Bonjour.*'

Arlette the nurse was standing by his bed grinning.

'Welcome to another day in the oldest hospital of Paris,' she said. 'In 1813, some of Napoleon's troops have been treated here for battle wands.'

'Wounds,' said Thomas. 'Battle wounds.'

Arlette grinned again.

'Wounds,' she said. '*Bien*. Thank you.'

'In Australia,' said Thomas, 'we treat our battle wounds with jam.'

Arlette frowned.

'Jam,' she said slowly.

Thomas gave her a thumbs up.

'Thank you,' said Arlette with another grin.

'Thank you,' said Thomas as she bustled out of the room.

Fantastic.

Only a tiny twinge from his chest.

I'm so lucky to have a nurse like Arlette, thought Thomas. I bet not many nurses would let a patient tell them lies just so they can test their English and the patient can test his nipples.

Thomas sipped his breakfast orange juice and wondered if any other doubters had ever been in this hospital. And whether, when their sickness got on top of them, they'd ever fainted and thought they were dying but woke up here instead, almost cured.

'G'day.'

Thomas looked up and grinned.

'How's it going?' said Holly, sitting on the edge of his bed and handing him a bunch of grapes.

'You look cured,' said Kevin, tossing him a bag of jelly snakes.

'I am,' said Thomas. 'Almost.'

Holly and Kevin glanced at each other, then both looked closely at Thomas.

'Chickens don't lay eggs,' said Kevin. 'They lay sausages.'

The three of them waited.

Thomas concentrated on his nipples.

'Just a tiny tickle in the left one,' he said. 'Hardly anything in the right one.'

'Brilliant,' said Holly.

'Test me again,' said Thomas. 'A harder test.'

Holly thought for a moment.

'Kevin's brought a teddy bear with him on this trip,' she said.

'Hey,' protested Kevin. 'We said we wouldn't use that one.'

Thomas concentrated.

'Same as before,' he said after a while. 'Just tiny tickles.'

'Brilliant,' said Holly.

'That's because it's not a bear,' said Kevin. 'It's a rabbit.'

Thomas gave Holly and Kevin a grateful smile. At this rate, by tomorrow he'd be completely cured.

He opened the jelly snakes to celebrate.

'G'day, love.'

Mum and Dad came into the room.

They both kissed Thomas. He hugged them back.

'Good news,' said Mum. 'The doctors say you can leave hospital today.'

'All your medical tests are clear,' said Dad. 'Your immune system's taken a bit of a bashing, but the doctors reckon it's already starting to fix itself.'

'We showed them the stuff from Vera Poulet,' said Mum. 'But they didn't really take it very seriously.'

'Immuno-epidemiologists,' said Kevin. 'What would they know?'

'The important thing,' said Dad to Thomas, 'is that you're on the mend. Whatever the virus or infection was that was making your thinking go a bit wonky, the doctors reckon you've given it the flick.'

Thomas didn't say anything.

It was a lot for Mum and Dad to get used to, this whole doubter thing. They were still digesting Nan's great-uncle Aaron and his itchy teeth.

Give them time.

'That's really good news about the tests, Mr and Mrs Gulliver,' Holly was saying.

She turned to Thomas and gave him the best smile he'd ever seen. Even her hair looked delighted.

Mum and Dad pulled up a couple of chairs and sat down close to the bed.

'Love,' said Mum to Thomas. 'Now you're better, there's something me and Dad want to say to you.'

For a fleeting moment, Thomas wondered if they were going to tell him off for not letting them know earlier about his lie-detector nipples.

'We've had a long talk,' said Mum, 'and we want to thank you.'

'You did a wonderful thing,' said Dad. 'Clearing the air like that. Bringing everything out in the open. Thank you, son. We're proud of you.'

Thomas was feeling a bit dizzy again, but in a good way.

'You've taught us a really important lesson, Thomas,' said Mum. 'People in families should tell each other the truth. Right, Brian?'

Dad nodded.

'What about people in beauty salons?' said

Kevin. 'Should they tell each other the truth too?'

Even though he was a bit light-headed, Thomas felt a strong urge to stuff a hospital mattress into Kevin's mouth.

But Mum just laughed.

'You're right, Kevin,' she said. 'People in beauty salons should tell the truth too. And if I ever have another one, I will only ever tell the truth there. In fact let's all agree that from now on, we're all going to tell the truth.'

They all shook hands.

Thomas flopped back onto his pillows, grinning happily.

'Oh,' said Mum. 'There is one other thing. We've had a call from the TV company in London that makes the English version of *Liar Liar*. They want to send somebody over to Paris to do a bit of publicity with us all. But we said only if you feel up to it, Thomas.'

'No problem,' said Thomas. 'Sounds like fun.'

Then he saw that Holly was looking uncertain.

He was about to ask her why, when Dad leaned forward.

'Champ,' he said quietly. 'Best not say anything to the English TV people about your nipples. If they believe all that doubter stuff, they might think you cheated when you were on the show and tell the producers back home.'

Thomas stared at Dad, a horrible feeling curdling inside him.

'It's not lying,' said Mum. 'It's just not saying anything.'

Thomas felt dizzy.

Not in a good way.

But the worst thing wasn't the dizziness or the sick feeling inside him, it was that his nipples felt like they were being attacked by large mosquitoes with very tickly leg hairs.

21

The hotel bed was even more comfortable than the hospital one, but Thomas couldn't relax.

He knew it wasn't the mattress.

It was the really difficult choice he had to make.

Jail or death.

Either confess to the English TV people in the morning and get dragged off to a juvenile correction facility, or keep quiet and wait for the sickness to kill him.

'There's only one way I'll get cured,' said Thomas turning to Holly and Kevin. 'Vera Poulet said the lies have to stop. All of them. That means I have to confess.'

'No,' said Holly. 'There's got to be another way.' She sat up in her bed and clicked her lamp on. 'Maybe you'll be cured if you just pay the money back.'

Thomas smiled sadly.

'Remember what the *Liar Liar* compere

announced when I won the big prize?' he said. 'About this trip being worth fifty thousand dollars. Where am I going to get fifty thousand dollars?'

He could see from Holly's face that if she had it, she'd give it to him.

'I know where you can get fifty thousand dollars,' said Kevin, sitting up in his bed. 'Listen to this.'

He grabbed one of Vera Poulet's photocopied research pages.

'It says here that in 1592 a Dutch girl saved her country with her eyebrows. The king of Belgium said he wasn't going to invade but when the girl's eyebrows went twitchy she knew he was lying and warned everyone.'

'Your point being?' said Holly.

'I've been thinking,' said Kevin. 'Maybe Thomas should be using his powers a bit more while he's still got them. Warn a few countries about invasions and stuff. They'd probably pay us big bucks. Fifty thousand at least.'

Holly sighed.

'It was just an idea,' said Kevin.

Thomas sighed too.

'No,' he said. 'I've got to confess.'

'You can't,' said Holly. 'The TV people will make an example of you. They'll have to. There are versions of *Liar Liar* produced in fourteen different countries. All those producers will want you punished really badly to make their shows look honest. You can't tell the TV people the truth.'

Thomas couldn't help smiling.

Look who was saying this. Holly Maxwell, the person who told Miss Pearson the truth about the project she'd forgotten to set. The person who told the ladies in the salon the truth about her back pimples.

'It's not just you who'll get into trouble,' said Holly. 'Your mum and dad could be arrested too.'

'I'll sign a legal document,' said Thomas. 'I'll swear they had nothing to do with it.'

Holly slumped back onto her bed.

Then she sat up again.

'Maybe it doesn't have to be every single lie,' she said. 'Maybe if you confess all your other lies, you can get away with this one.'

Thomas frowned.

'What other lies?' he said.

He couldn't think of any.

Holly flicked her eyes towards Kevin, who was still reading.

'Parents,' she mouthed.

Thomas stared at her. Then he realised what she meant. She was talking about the time Kevin's mum forgot Kevin's version of *Stairway To Heaven* and then lied about being as proud of Kevin as all their other kids. Thomas and Holly had talked about it afterwards and decided not to say anything to Kevin.

That was a sort of lie.

Thomas didn't want to say anything now.

He wanted to get cured, but not if it was going

to make a friend feel really bad.

'My parents?' said Kevin, sitting up. 'What about my parents?'

'Nothing,' said Thomas.

He flinched as his nipples went itchy.

'Oh, you mean the phone call,' said Kevin.

'What phone call?' said Thomas.

'I was going to tell you,' said Kevin. 'While you were in hospital my mum and dad rang me from Australia, even though it was the middle of the night there, because they were missing me so much.'

Thomas waited for his nipples to go itchy again.

He hoped they wouldn't.

They didn't.

'It was great,' said Kevin. 'They didn't care how much it cost. We talked for more than an hour.'

Thomas's nipples stayed itch-free.

He smiled.

'That must have been really good,' he said to Kevin.

'Yeah,' said Kevin. 'Next trip I probably won't need a teddy. I mean rabbit.'

Thomas saw that Holly was smiling too. Then her eyes went sad and concerned. Her hair looked sad and concerned too.

'So you're going to do it?' she said quietly to Thomas. 'Confess to the TV people?'

Thomas nodded and flopped back onto his pillow.

'It's really late,' he said. 'We'd better go to sleep.'

But he couldn't, not for a long time. He lay staring into the darkness, listening to Holly softly breathing and Kevin snuffling.

He felt scared, but he knew now that only the truth could save him.

The lies in his family were all out in the open, and all forgiven.

All except one.

22

Gerard the English TV publicity executive was very enthusiastic.

'*Magnifique,*' he kept saying.

He said it a lot during the happy-family pillow fight in Mum and Dad's hotel room. Six times he got them to have the pillow fight so the camera crew could film the excitement from different angles and show the world what a fun prize a *Liar Liar* trip was.

'*Magnifique,*' he shouted, even when Dad got carried away and knocked Kevin off the bed and into a suitcase.

Thomas didn't think it was very *magnifique*. Each time he plucked up the courage and was about to confess to being a liar and a cheat and a criminal, he got whacked round the head with a pillow.

It was just as bad in the hotel pool.

Gerard got them all to have a happy-family frolic in the shallow end.

'*Formidable*,' he yelled enthusiastically as he peered into the video screen on the camera.

Thomas screwed up his eyes because of all the splashing. He screwed up his courage as well. The pillow fight had left his head feeling not good, so he daren't wait any longer.

He knew exactly what he was going to say.

Gerard, I have something to confess. When I appeared on Liar Liar, *my nipples gave me an unfair advantage and I cheated. If I promise never to do it again, will you be really kind and not tell the police?*

Thomas turned to Gerard and opened his mouth to speak.

Before he could, Kevin opened his mouth and spoke first.

'I think it's a bit soon for me to be swimming after breakfast and a pillow fight,' said Kevin, and threw up in the water.

'*Superbe*,' yelled Gerard as they all posed on the steps in front of Notre Dame cathedral.

Do it now, Thomas said to himself. This is the last bit of filming. Speak up.

But he felt so ill he wasn't sure if he could.

Holly was giving him worried looks. Kevin was making talking movements with his hands.

Thomas tried to breathe more slowly, to quell the sickness and dizziness that were creeping back. His head had been aching all day. His nipples had been agitated since breakfast when Kevin told the waiter that muesli in Australia came with bits of kangaroo poo in it.

'Thomas,' yelled Gerard. 'Look up. Be *content*. Be *trés content*.'

Thomas looked up.

High above him, a row of stone heads were grimacing down from the front of the cathedral. Gargoyles, a nearby tourist guide was calling them. Thomas couldn't tell if they were human or animal, but their expressions were very miserable.

That's how I'll probably look, he thought. As I'm being put into the police van.

Then, as Thomas stared at them some more, the expression on the gargoyle faces made him think of something else.

All the doubters through the centuries who hadn't been cured.

Poor kids, he thought. What chance did they have?

He wished he could go back into history and save them all. Make their families tell the truth. But he couldn't. There was only one doubter he could help now.

Slowly Thomas made his way down the steps.

'Thomas, this is not so *superbe*,' said Gerard.

Thomas chose a place where everybody could see and hear him. Gerard and the camera crew. Mum and Dad and Holly and Kevin. The tourists taking photos of the cathedral.

'I lied,' he said as loudly as he could.

Mum and Dad were coming down the steps now,

looking so concerned that Thomas hesitated.

But only for a moment.

'I didn't win this trip fairly,' said Thomas. 'I used my itchy nipples.'

He could see Holly and Kevin were looking pretty tense too.

Gerard was looking confused.

'Nipples?' he said.

'Nipples,' said Thomas so loudly a group of tourists moved away in alarm. 'I used them to win. I only pretended I was guessing. It was all lies.'

'Of course it was all lies,' said Gerard, smiling. 'You're the *Liar Liar* champion of Australia. *Magnifique.*'

Thomas yelled at Gerard in exasperation.

'I cheated.'

Gerard stopped smiling.

'Eh?' he said.

'Mum and Dad didn't know anything about this,' said Thomas. 'Whatever severe legal punishment is going to happen, it should only happen to me.'

'And me,' said Holly.

She stepped forward and stood next to Thomas.

'No,' he said, trying to nudge her away.

'I knew Thomas was cheating,' said Holly. 'I could have stopped him, but I didn't because he's my friend and he was trying to save his life.'

Thomas was stunned. Holly was trying to share his punishment.

'No,' he said again.

She put her hand over his mouth.

Kevin stepped forward and stood next to them both.

'Cheating was my idea,' he said. 'I made Thomas do it. I was hoping he could get a trip to Paris to cure his rare historical disease. And win some jet skis with harpoons.'

There was a long silence.

Thomas watched Gerard, who didn't look confused any more, pull out his mobile phone and dial.

He knew Gerard was probably calling the police. He knew things probably wouldn't be very pleasant from now on.

But he didn't care. His head was starting to feel better already. All of him was.

As Mum and Dad each put an arm round him, Thomas looked up at the stone gargoyle faces again and sent a silent message to Vera Poulet.

Thank you.

'Don't worry, son,' said Dad. 'Me and Mum won't let the TV mob do anything to you.'

'If they want to get legal,' said Mum, 'they can get legal with me and Dad. I know a lawyer with bushy eyebrows.'

Thomas stared at Mum and Dad. For a brief moment he had a wonderful vision.

Mum and Dad in an old people's home, not letting anyone take their biscuits.

Then Thomas realised that Gerard didn't sound

like a person talking to the police.

'Tristan,' Gerard was saying into his phone. 'I'm ditching the Paris shoot. The kid's got some sort of medical complaint. Possibly a mental condition. Is that Canadian prizewinner still in Venice with her family? *Magnifique*. I'll fly down there and use them.'

As Thomas nestled into Mum and Dad, he felt his head clearing and his weariness vanishing and the sickness slipping away and his nipples becoming calm and peaceful.

He gave Holly and Kevin the best smile he'd given anyone for a long time.

He was cured.

23

It was the best surprise picnic Thomas had ever been on.

'More jam, anyone?' said Mum.

'Delicious, love,' said Dad, sprawled out on his back and sighing contentedly up at the evening sky. 'But no more scones for me, thanks. I'm going to have some cake.'

'Me too, please,' said Holly, grinning.

'And me,' said Kevin. 'I love cake. I ate twenty-three slices at a birthday party once and threw up.'

'Hmmm,' said Mum to Kevin. 'I think it might be just as well Thomas doesn't get itchy nipples any more.'

Kevin looked indignant.

'It's true,' he said. 'I did throw up. Ask Rocco Fusilli's parents.'

Thomas grinned.

'I was there,' he said.

'If Thomas still got itchy nipples,' said Alisha,

'he'd have got them this afternoon when Theo arrived to collect me in that ute he reckons can do three hundred ks an hour.'

They all laughed.

Except Alisha.

'Theo's worse than Garth,' she said crossly. 'One day I'll meet a boy who doesn't make things up.'

Thomas smiled fondly at his sister.

She scowled back at him, then winked.

Thomas felt good. His head was still clear and his nipples were still normal. Even the jetlag from the flight back wasn't worrying him, or the roar of the trucks over in the Koala Reserve Industrial Estate.

'OK, everyone,' said Dad, sitting up. 'Tomorrow me and Mum will be out looking for new jobs, so before we get too busy, I want to propose a toast.'

'Hear, hear,' said Mum.

Dad cleared his throat and topped up his tea.

'Thomas gave us more than a trip to Paris,' said Dad. 'He gave us more than a new car or a pair of jet skis. He gave us so much I can't put it all into words.'

Dad paused and raised his cup and looked at Thomas for a long time.

'Let me put it this way,' he said finally. 'We're a family again.'

Mum gave Thomas a grateful smile, and her eyes were almost as glowing as Holly's.

Holly, Kevin and Alisha applauded.

Thomas felt his nipples starting to itch, but it was only ordinary old embarrassment.

Oops, he thought, time to change the subject.

'Look at that beautiful sunset,' he said.

They all gazed at it.

It was one of the best things Thomas had seen in his life. In front of them the municipal gardens tumbled down a steep slope to the base of the squash courts, above which the tower, the local mobile-phone one, soared into the pink and orange smog-streaked sky.

'That is so gorgeous,' sighed Mum, and put her arms round Dad.

Thomas saw Holly and Kevin grinning at him and he knew they were thinking the same as him.

Better than Paris.

Thomas nodded and grinned back.

He gazed up at the very tip of the tower, where a distant but bright mobile-phone advertising sign was slowly flashing on and off.

It was nothing compared to what Thomas could feel glowing inside him.

The happiest feeling he'd ever had.

It made every part of his body tingle except his nipples.

True.

Teacher's Pet

'Ginger, Ginger, Ginger,' said Mr Napier. 'How did a nice family like yours end up with a person like you in it?'

Morris GLEITZMAN

Teacher's Pet

'A brilliantly funny writer' — Sunday Telegraph

Trouble seems to follow Ginger around, especially as her best friend is a fierce-looking stray dog.

'Morris Gleitzman has a rare gift for writing very funny stories' - *Guardian*

'Readers can't get enough of him' - *Independent*

Two Weeks with the Queen

Colin Mudford is on a quest. His brother, Luke, has cancer and the doctors in Australia don't seem to be able to cure him. Colin reckons it's up to him to find the best doctor in the world.

How better to do this than asking the Queen to help . . . ?

'A gem of a book' - *Guardian*

'One of the best books I've ever read. I wish I had written it' - Paula Danziger

puffin.co.uk   morrisgleitzman.com

Join Limpy the cane toad in three hilarious, heroic adventures

TOAD RAGE TOAD HEAVEN TOAD AWAY

Illustrations © Moira Millman

From the Sydney Olympics to the Amazon jungle, Limpy just can't help getting into some sticky situations.

Be warned – it could get messy!

puffin.co.uk

morrisgleitzman.com